Whoa. Olivia felt as if her eyeballs were bouncing back and forth like tennis balls over a net as she looked from Amelia to Finn and back again. Even now that Amelia had managed to force a scowl, she and Finn were still staring at each other. It was as if they couldn't look away.

There is some serious crushing going on, Olivia thought. *Between the leaders of the two groups who seem to hate each other the most!*

Sink your fangs into these:

MY SISTER THE VAMPIRE

Switched

Fangtastic!

Revamped!

Vampalicious

Take Two

Love Bites

Lucky Break

Star Style

Twin Spins!

Date with Destiny

Flying Solo

Stake Out!

Double Disaster!

MY BROTHER THE WEREWOLF

Cry Wolf!

Puppy Love!

Howl-oween!

Sienna Mercer

My Sister the Vampire

Flipping Out!

EGMONT

With special thanks to Stephanie Burgis

For Freya, with love

EGMONT
We bring stories to life

My Sister the Vampire: Flipping Out! first published in Great Britain 2013
by Egmont UK Limited
The Yellow Building, 1 Nicholas Road
London W11, 4AN

Created by Working Partners Limited, London WC1X 9HH

ISBN 978 1 4052 6571 3

5 7 9 10 8 6 4

www.egmont.co.uk

A CIP catalogue record for this title is available from the British Library

54092/5

Typeset by Avon DataSet Ltd, Bidford on Avon, Warwickshire B49 6QA
Printed and bound in Great Britain by the CPI Group

Chapter One

'You must be like water . . . running water . . .'

Ivy Vega clamped one hand over her mouth to hold back a snicker. *I can't let myself laugh*, she told herself. *It's not fair!*

Mr Abbott was sleeping in the front seat of the Vegas' car after a red-eye flight from London. Unfortunately, he was having a deep conversation with a martial arts student – in his sleep.

'Flowww,' he mumbled. His chin sagged over his bright orange 'I ❤ London' T-shirt, muffling his words. '. . . like a waaaterfall . . .'

'If there was a prize for Most Jet-Lagged Man in the World,' Ivy whispered to her twin, 'he would have to win!'

Olivia Abbott stifled a giggle, her blue eyes bright. 'No competition!' she whispered back. 'Do you think we should we call the *Guinness Book of World Records*?'

'Well . . .' Ivy eyed the London Eye ferris wheel pictured on Olivia's babydoll T-shirt and grinned. With a quick side-glance at their bio-dad in the driving seat of the car, she lowered her voice. 'Maybe I should call a few gossip magazines first!'

Olivia rolled her eyes. 'What are you talking about?'

'Ahem?' Letting a grin spread across her face, Ivy pointed to the heart that had been drawn in pink ink around one of the pods on the ferris wheel on Olivia's shirt. 'Does that or does that not say *JC + OA*?'

Olivia's cheeks flushed pink. Still, her lips curved into a tiny smile. 'So?'

'So-o-o . . .' Ivy drawled, and nudged her twin. 'I'm guessing that *someone* had a romantic moment with her boyfriend on the London Eye. And since that boyfriend just happens to be a major movie star, I'm betting the magazines would be *fascinated* to hear that.'

'Oh, shush, you!' Olivia batted at Ivy's shoulder, but she couldn't hide her smile.

Ivy batted right back at her, laughing with delight.

Olivia's tourist T-shirt was one more reminder of just how far away she had been – but now that she was home, everything finally felt right again to Ivy. From the grin on Olivia's face – and the heart she'd drawn on her T-shirt! – it looked like everything was going right for Olivia, too.

Ivy's sister gave an impatient bounce as she

turned to look at her adoptive parents, who were snoring loudly in the backseat. 'I can't believe they're both sleeping. I have *never* felt so awake!'

Ivy rolled her eyes. 'Tell me about it. You've been fidgeting ever since you got here!' But her smile was affectionate as she gazed at her twin.

The Abbotts had flown to London a week ago so that Olivia could film scenes for the upcoming Hollywood film *Eternal Sunset*. Now Olivia should have been crashing, after being up all night on the plane ride home. But between the hectic filming schedule she had just gone through, her crazy levels of jet lag, and her giddy happiness over her reunion with Jackson, she was acting exactly like a bumble bee that had rolled in sugar. Ivy had never seen her twin so hyper.

'Ooh! I almost forgot!' Olivia let out a squeak of excitement, diving down to grab the bag from between her glittering pink tennis shoes. 'I have *gifts*! I got you guys so many souvenirs.'

'Just wait!' Laughing, Ivy put one hand on her twin's arm. 'It's too cramped in here for gift-giving. Plus, Dad's busy driving, and your parents are out like lights. Why don't you hand them out when we get home to Undertaker Hill?'

'You're right. Of course you're right.' Nodding firmly, Olivia gave another little bounce. 'We *should* build suspense. That way, we'll all enjoy the pay-off even more when it comes!'

'Is this movie-talk?' Ivy raised her eyebrows, thinking of Olivia's cinema-obsessed best friend Camilla. 'I think you're the first of us to get fluent in Camilla-ese!'

Before Olivia could reply, her adoptive father lurched forwards in his seat.

Still asleep, he bellowed, '*Forget* shape and structure! They have no meaning he-ahhhhhzzz . . .'

His last word was swallowed by an enormous

snore as his head fell back against the seat.

Ivy and Olivia both had to cover their mouths to hold back their giggles. Even Charles Vega, in the front of the car, looked as if he was choking back a laugh.

'Welcome home,' Ivy whispered to her sister, giving her a hug.

Back at Ivy's house, her dad and stepmom, Lillian, laid out a light breakfast for the returning trio. Even cereal and toast didn't seem to be enough to fight the jet lag, though. Mrs Abbott had to excuse herself to go upstairs after less than five minutes.

'I need to splash some water on my face,' she said. 'Maybe that'll wake me up.'

'Of course,' Lillian said. 'Please make yourself at home.' As Mrs Abbott walked out of the room, Lillian turned to Olivia and Mr Abbott. 'Won't you two tell me about your flight?'

'Well . . .' Olivia began. Then she stopped, as Mr Abbott's head suddenly lolled forwards.

Ivy gasped as he began to fall face first into his cereal bowl . . .

. . . Only to catch himself just in time. He jerked back as he grunted awake, sending his silver spoon flying through the air, too high and fast for any human to catch.

But none of the Vegas were human.

Charles Vega's hand flashed up with vampire speed and snatched the spoon from mid-air.

Uh-oh. Ivy stared at her father. *That was a mistake. A real human couldn't have done that!*

Next to Charles, Lillian was visibly wincing, while Olivia looked just as alarmed as Ivy felt. Talk about a vampire giveaway! Even Charles seemed to realise his mistake. He gave the spoon in his hand a stern glance, looking as annoyed as if he'd found a shoe in his closet that wasn't perfectly polished.

Luckily, Mr Abbott was clearly too zonked to have noticed. *There's one advantage of jet lag,* Ivy thought ruefully. *It keeps you from noticing the vampires all around you!*

'Whew.' Mrs Abbott walked back into the room, her face still pink and damp-looking. 'I can't believe how tired I am.'

'I can imagine.' Lillian Vega smiled sympathetically. 'I've been on enough red-eye flights for my own movie jobs. I know *exactly* how difficult jet lag can be.'

'Do you know, I'm so exhausted, I'm actually having hallucinations.' Mrs Abbott collapsed back on to her stool at the breakfast bar, rubbing her eyes. 'As I was walking past Ivy's room, I could have sworn I saw a coffin inside!'

Oops. I must have forgotten to close my bedroom

door. 'Ha! Ha.' Ivy almost choked on her forced laughter. 'Just imagine! A coffin in a bedroom. Isn't that funny?'

But she cringed at the look her father gave her. This one was the look he had when something *really* serious went wrong, like a stain on one of his silk shirts.

'What were you thinking?' Olivia hissed into her ear. 'You know you need to keep your door locked when you have "bunny-company" around the house!'

'Did you just say something about bunnies, sweetheart?' Mrs Abbott frowned at Olivia as she picked up her last piece of toast. 'Or was I imagining that, too?'

Olivia's cheeks flushed. 'Umm . . .'

Her adoptive mother stared at her. 'Why would you be talking to Ivy about rabbits?'

Lillian leaned forwards, gracious as always, to

rescue the situation. 'You must tell me,' she said to Mrs Abbott, 'what did you think of London's sights?'

'Oh, *London* . . .' Mrs Abbott gave a sigh of delight. 'It was amazing. The culture! The architecture! The –'

'I'll just clear up,' Ivy mumbled, as she felt her dad's disapproving gaze lingering on her.

'I'll help.' Olivia bounced to her feet. 'I can't sit still anyway!'

'Thanks.' As Ivy started gathering up plates, she gave her dad an apologetic look. 'Sorry,' she said in a low voice, aiming her words at both him and Olivia. 'It's been such a crazy time, I'm just a little absent-minded right now.'

Olivia's adoptive parents might be wonderful people, but they were still bunnies – humans who weren't in on the vampire secret – and they could never be allowed to find out. Under normal circumstances, she wouldn't have forgotten to close the door of her bedroom.

Ivy had just started high school, though . . . and the circumstances were anything but 'normal'.

Olivia's energy seemed to dim a bit for the first time since she'd arrived. 'Is high school really as tough as you said in our Lonely Echo chats?'

'Just wait until tomorrow,' Ivy told her, as Charles joined in with the others' conversation. 'You'll see for yourself. And wait until the homework starts rolling in – you'll need to learn how to write while wearing gloves!'

Olivia blinked, then shook her head. 'OK, it can't just be jet lag. That comment made *no* sense at all.'

'Trust me.' Ivy leaned close to whisper in her twin's ear. 'Even my RHP' – *Rapid Healing Process* – 'struggles to keep up with all the paper-cuts I'm getting from the mountains of essays.'

'Ouch.' Olivia sighed as she picked up the last of the plates. 'Well, I'm still not dreading the new school . . . but I really wish I could take a day off to recover after all my travelling.'

'What?!' Charles and Mrs Abbott both broke off at once to turn on Olivia.

'You cannot afford to miss any more schooling,' they both declared.

Poor Olivia, Ivy thought. She had to force herself to hold back a smile at the look on her twin's face. *That's the real downside of having four parents. Even more people to lecture you.*

The voices woke Mr Abbott at last. He let out a grunt like a startled bear. 'Uhh! Sorry. Sorry.' Yawning, he stumbled to his feet. 'I don't quite seem to be able to fight this jet lag. It's like a mysterious opponent that hides in shadows and cannot be overcome by force.'

'We noticed,' said Mrs Abbott. Sighing, she

traded a meaningful look with Lillian.

'Well, then, if no one minds . . .' Mr Abbott stepped back from the breakfast bar, stretching out his arms in a warming-up pose. 'I'll just stand up and do some "forms". That will definitely keep me awake.'

It'll keep all of us awake, Ivy thought. She looked down, biting her lip to keep from laughing. *Ouch!* Her lip stung. *It's definitely time to get my fangs filed.* She'd skipped an appointment at the vampire dentist so that she could be here this morning, but she hadn't rescheduled yet. *I can't forget to do that!* The First Law of the Night demanded that vampires kept their existence secret – so every vampire had to get their teeth regularly filed to keep them at a normal, human length.

But how could Ivy think about practicalities when there was a middle-aged man doing kung-fu mimes in her kitchen? Every sensible plan in her head fizzled away as she gaped at the sight before her. *What on earth could that move be?* she wondered. *Man fumbling for a light switch? Man tearing down cobwebs, maybe?*

Even Lillian, who was always perfectly poised in social situations, looked bemused.

Olivia broke the awkward silence. 'Time for presents!' She dived under the breakfast bar to grab her bag, hitting her head against the bottom of the counter.

'Look out!' Ivy reached down to help her twin up. Jet lag finally seemed to have hit Olivia, who was starting to weave slightly from side to side. 'I'm sure it can wait just a little –'

'Absolutely not!' Olivia emerged with the sequinned purple bag, looking tousled but pleased with herself. 'I don't want to keep you guys in suspense any longer. A pay-off is only good if the audience still wants it, you know!'

'I really will have to learn Camilla-ese now that you're in the movie business, won't I?' Ivy gave a mock-sigh, shaking her head. 'Can I buy a phrase book somewhere, at least?'

'Oh, you'll pick it up as we go,' Olivia said breezily. Fumbling slightly, she put the bag on the table and opened it up to rummage through the chaos inside. 'And for you, Ivy, from London . . . ta-da!'

Ivy blinked in disbelief. *Is that a teddy bear?*

It was. It was a small stuffed bear in a red raincoat and blue felt hat. Olivia beamed as she held it out. 'To keep you company in your coff– . . . erm, bed!'

'Uh, thanks.' Eyebrows raised, Ivy accepted the bear. *She must have been really Jackson-giddy when she bought these souvenirs. At least I should be grateful it isn't pink!*

Chapter Two

Here we go. Olivia braced herself as she stood in the doorway to Franklin Grove High School. *This is going to be great*, she repeated in her head. *I've been waiting for this all summer!*

She looked down at her carefully chosen outfit. Her glittery pink short-sleeved shirt, with its shiny Union Jack in the centre, was her very favourite British souvenir, and it looked perfect with her paler pink capris. *I'm all set!*

Unfortunately, her stomach didn't seem to be listening to her head. First it did a nervous front-flip. Then a backflip! Olivia swallowed hard.

I've performed whole cheerleading routines with fewer flips and tumbles than my belly is doing right now!

Olivia took a deep breath and turned to look at her sister. *As long as I'm with Ivy, it'll all be fine.*

But Ivy was groaning as she gazed into the dimly-lit front hallway of Franklin Grove High. 'You see?' she muttered to Olivia. 'I told you this was Bizarro World.'

As Olivia followed her twin into the school, she was forced to agree. Her head whipped back and forth as she tried to take in everything she saw in the crowded hallway. And what an unexpected crowd it was . . .

Wow. The goths really were in charge here! Goth girls and boys lined the walls, leaning against the lockers with their arms crossed, wearing sunglasses despite the low light. Other goths slouched in groups down the centre of the hallway while the few bunnies leaped to the side to make way for them, nearly squeaking with panic as they approached. And then there were the skaters . . .

'So, are you freaked out yet?' said Ivy, giving Olivia a nudge.

'Well . . .' Olivia shrugged, settling her own nerves. 'It can't be more of a mix here than the kind I saw on the film set. The actors and the crew members all got along just fine, no matter how different they were. In fact . . .' She dropped her voice. 'I'm pretty sure the actress who played Jackson's mom was secretly dating the key grip!'

'The *what*?' Ivy stared at her. 'She was dating a *key*? Or a glove? How did that even work?'

Oops. Olivia shook her head ruefully. 'Sorry. Technical term. Maybe I should have saved that bit of gossip for Camilla?'

'Maybe,' Ivy agreed. 'But you can do that later.

Right now . . .' She drew a deep breath, looking even paler than usual. Her lips twisted. 'It's time to face the music!' Squaring her shoulders, she headed into the crowd.

Why does she look like she's heading into battle? Olivia wondered. As she walked by her sister's side, her concern deepened. *Something is seriously wrong.* Normally, Ivy looked so confident as she walked around. She never cared about other people's opinions. But here . . . she looked tense. Her eyes darted everywhere, as if she were afraid of being attacked.

And maybe she had a point. As they headed for their lockers together, every head turned to watch them. Olivia didn't need vampire hearing to pick up the whispers rising all around them.

'Is that Ivy's *twin*?'

'That's not possible! She's so . . . *pink*!'

'Geez, look at her skin-tone. Why would she put on a fake tan like that?'

'Maybe it's not fake.'

'Then how could she have let it *happen*?'

Gritting her teeth, Olivia hung on to the shoulder strap of her sequinned bag and forced herself not to react. *They're not really making fun of me*, she told herself. *They're just confused. And why wouldn't they be? Ivy and I must be the least alike identical twins in the world!*

She wasn't the only one hearing the whispers. As Ivy came to a stop in front of her locker, Olivia could see the frustration on her twin's face.

'Are you OK?' Ivy muttered.

'I'm fine.' Olivia gave her a reassuring smile.

Knowing how protective Ivy was, she guessed her sister had probably wanted to stop and shout at every single person who'd whispered about Olivia on the way. As sweet as that was,

Olivia couldn't let it happen.

Unlike the students at Franklin Grove Middle School, Lincoln Vale kids hadn't grown up with vampires. The Franklin Grove vamps had to work extra hard here to keep their secret safe. That meant: *Make no waves!*

'It's just going to take a while to get used to, that's all,' Olivia said firmly.

'Good luck with that,' Ivy grumbled. 'I've been here a week already, and I'm not getting used to anything!'

'Oh, come on.' Olivia gave her twin a sympathetic smile. 'There's got to be something good about this school, right? I mean . . .' she looked around the dimly lit hallway, searching for something positive to say '. . . at least the light isn't bright enough to hurt your eyes.'

Ivy snorted. 'I wish . . . oh, no!'

'What is it?' As her sister's eyes widened with

horror, Olivia twisted around . . . just in time to see half a dozen goths descend in a mass of black hair, flapping black trench coats and jangling silver jewellery.

They swept down around Ivy like a flock of blackbirds.

'Oh, Ivy, where did you get that *killer* ensemble?' The girl in front was almost shrieking with excitement, reaching out to stroke Ivy's Pall Bearers T-shirt with one black-nailed hand.

Olivia watched Ivy squint – not in one of her patented death-stares this time, but in an obvious attempt to hide the fact that she was rolling her eyes as she scooted backwards.

'These are the exact same clothes I was wearing last Friday,' she said, sighing. 'There's nothing special about them.'

'Ohhhh!' breathed the girl who'd asked the question. She clapped one hand to her mouth, her eyes widening in obvious wonder. 'That is so daring of you!'

The two girls behind Olivia started whispering frantically.

'She's so cool, she doesn't even do laundry!'

'I'm going to try that, too!'

More and more goths gravitated towards them, as if Ivy were a magnet pulling them in from throughout the school. Olivia had never seen anything like it. Her twin had no choice but to keep backing away to create room for the newcomers. Within a few minutes, she had somehow drifted from one side of the hall to the other, fending off fashion-related questions with every step.

'But how do you get *so* pale?' the closest girl asked imploringly. 'I want to do it, too!'

'Um . . .' Ivy gave Olivia a look of obvious desperation, but they were separated by so many goths now, Olivia could only shrug sympathetically.

'I don't know,' Ivy said. 'Just luck?'

The girl pressed on, forcing Ivy further backwards. 'But what brand of pale foundation do you use? You can tell me, Ivy! I'd never tell anyone else!'

'I don't really . . .' Ivy began.

As she backed away, she walked straight into a sweet-faced bunny girl who was trying to edge past the group of goths. It would have been bad enough if Ivy was human – but with her vampire strength, she knocked the girl straight to the ground.

Oh, no! Olivia raced over to help. Ivy was already apologising as she leaned over the bunny girl.

'I'm so sorry!' Ivy said, for at least the third time. 'I wasn't looking where I was going. Are you OK?'

Olivia and Ivy took an arm each as they helped the girl to her feet. But the bunny shrugged them off.

'No, no!' she said to Ivy. 'Please don't apologise. It was *my* fault. I totally should have been watching where you were going! *No one* should get in your way. Ever!'

Hey. Suddenly frowning, Olivia let go of her arm. *She didn't have to be nasty about it.* That kind of cruel sarcasm had been exactly what their old nemesis Charlotte Brown had specialised in, back at Franklin Grove Middle.

But as Olivia watched the other girl, the truth dawned on her. She wasn't being sarcastic at all. She actually thought the collision *was* somehow her fault.

'*Please* forgive me!' she said earnestly, gathering up the last of her books. 'I promise I won't do it again.'

'But . . .' Ivy began.

It was too late. Still apologising, the girl had already hurried away.

Olivia met Ivy's gaze and saw the desperate frustration simmering there. She started to step forwards but the goths had already moved back in. They swept between her and her twin like a tsunami. Olivia felt dizzy as she watched the wave carry Ivy down the hall. Even though she was standing still, it seemed like the world was spinning around her.

Ivy and Sophia were right. High school really is weird! Olivia was used to fangirls swooping down on Jackson and other movie stars. But on her own sister? Just for being *cool*?

Olivia took a deep breath and rubbed her eyes, trying to steady herself. But when she opened her eyes again, she saw the weirdest sight yet. Ivy's best friend Sophia was walking towards her down the hall, wearing one of her usual sleek black outfits . . . but her hair was . . . partially blonde!

It's so different, Olivia thought, staring. *But it's fabulous!*

Ivy had told her all about how Sophia had crushed on a skater-boy and gone pixie-blonde for a couple of days. The boy wasn't anywhere in sight now, but Olivia absolutely *loved* Sophia's new hair!

Sophia's black roots were already growing back, and she had obviously taken the opportunity to dye the tips of her hair the same colour, leaving jagged streaks of blonde in chaotic patterns all over her head. It looked a little bit like lightning!

'Hey, you!' Sophia's lips curved into a smile as she joined Olivia. 'You're back! How was London?'

'It was all great,' Olivia said weakly. She shook her head wonderingly even as she moved forwards for a welcome-back hug. 'But you . . . what about you? You look *amazing*. I love your hair!'

'Thanks. Me, too!' Sophia hugged Olivia. When she pulled back, Olivia could see her scanning the crowd of goths surrounding Ivy. 'I saw that little scene with the bunny girl, though. Is everyone here still sucking up to Ivy?'

'Oh, yes.' Olivia sighed as she stepped back. She could hardly bring herself to look at the disaster unfolding for her twin. How was Ivy, of all people, going to endure four years of this? Even now, one of the goth-girls was stroking Ivy's hair, and Ivy was visibly shuddering with displeasure. 'Maybe I should ask Jackson how *he* deals with all the attention,' Olivia murmured.

Then she grinned. *Hey, that's right! I get to talk to Jackson whenever I like, now.* After all their months apart, it still felt delicious to remember that they were finally a couple again.

Sophia cocked one eyebrow at her in a *Come on, now* look. 'Ivy may be popular, but she's not quite A-list yet.' She grinned mischievously. 'Besides, can you really see her using the classic Hollywood disguise of sunglasses and a baseball cap?'

'Hmm. Maybe not,' Olivia admitted.

As Sophia put her black faux-leather shoulder bag in her locker, Olivia looked around for her own locker. Her eyebrows scrunched together as she read the numbers. 61, 62, 63 . . . *Wait a minute. Where's 323?* She'd assumed her locker would be in the same area of the hall as all the others in her grade. But these numbers weren't anywhere near her own!

Frowning, she pulled out her cell phone. *Maybe I'm misremembering it.*

When she looked in her phone's message box,

though, she saw a second text from the school – a text she'd never actually read, in all the craziness of filming.

Drat. She sighed as she read the text. It turned out, because she had missed Week One of school, her locker wasn't with the other freshmen at all! Instead, it was further down – with the juniors and seniors.

Oh, well. Considering how pushy her fan club is, I wasn't going to get to hang out with Ivy anyway. Shrugging, Olivia put the phone in her backpack and stood on tiptoe to try to catch her twin's eye.

'*I'll see you in homeroom*,' she whispered. The crowd might be intense, but she knew her vampire twin would have no problem hearing her words. 'I have to go find my locker. It's not with yours.'

Ivy broke off from yet another fashion question – 'Honestly, I don't really *have* an opinion on whether purple lipstick "totally stakes" black lipstick!' – to wave back at her. 'See you later!' she called.

At that, Ivy's entire adoring crowd swung round to glare at Olivia. Every goth eyed her up and down with curled lips and frowns . . . then turned their attention back to Ivy.

Dismissed, Olivia realised. She gritted her teeth, forcing herself to keep her head high. *Whatever!*

Maybe Ivy's goth-fans didn't approve of her sparkly pink outfit, but that didn't stop it from being fabulous . . . right?

Right, she told herself firmly. But she couldn't help a small voice in her head from asking: *Why is Ivy staying with them even after she saw them do that?* Olivia had never seen her looking so helpless or so overwhelmed . . . but she *knew* her twin. Ivy was the strongest person she'd ever met. Why wasn't she just speaking her mind to her 'fans' and walking away? *She isn't secretly enjoying all this attention . . . is she?*

Olivia took a deep breath and forced the suspicion aside. Leaving Ivy and her fan club behind, she started down the hall, following the locker numbers higher. But she couldn't forget what she'd just seen. *Who knew Ivy would turn into Most Popular Girl at School?* she thought wryly. *Just wait for the yearbook!*

She had to weave her way through the mass of older goths in the hallway as she headed for the junior and senior lockers. *There really are a LOT of goths here*, she realised. *Does that explain why Ivy's so popular?*

As she waited for a space to clear, Olivia suddenly came face to face with the most gothabulous senior girl she'd ever seen . . . and the most confused-looking one, too. She looked Olivia up and down, shaking her head in amazement and making her heavy silver earrings jangle.

'Is something wrong?' Olivia asked.

'Oh, come on, Ivy,' the older goth-girl said. She crossed her arms over her leather jacket. 'Are you really *so* bothered by being liked that you've gone "alternatively" mainstream? Or did you just get into a wrestling match with a Glitter Goblin?'

Ouch! Olivia couldn't help glancing down at her sparkly top. *Maybe this isn't my favourite souvenir any more, after all.*

Then she took a deep breath. *Yes, it is*, she told herself. *Whatever this girl thinks of it!* Still, she found herself shifting her bag to cover it up as she answered, swallowing down her hurt for the second time that morning. 'Sorry for being so mainstream,' she said coolly, 'but that's because I'm *not* Ivy. I'm Olivia, Ivy's twin.'

'Oh.' The older girl stepped backwards, frowning. 'I'm Amelia Thompson.'

And you're not apologising for being rude, are you, Olivia thought. *Hmm* . . .

'Hey, you were in the newspapers, weren't you?' Amelia's eyes narrowed. 'Back when Jackson Caulfield came to town. You two are making *Eternal Sunset* now, right?'

Olivia smiled. Just thinking of Jackson was enough to make her lips stretch into a goofy grin. *My boyfriend* . . . she thought giddily. 'That's right!'

'Hmm.' Amelia's pale face hardened. 'That's one of my favourite books. I hope you guys don't mess it up.'

Olivia felt the smile stiffen on her face. 'I'll try my best not to,' she said.

Amelia didn't reply . . . and as Olivia gazed at the older girl, she wondered: was her expression actually supposed to be threatening? Or did she just *never* smile?

With an impatient sniff, Amelia swept past,

silver jewellery clanking and black-painted lips pursed. Olivia shook her head in bafflement.

What a weird encounter.

Ivy had said this school was *bizarre*. It was more than bizarre – it was . . . it was . . .

There's not even a word for it! Olivia decided.

Blowing out her breath, she pushed forwards to find her locker, weaving through a cluster of skater-boys on the way. Most of them ignored her as if she didn't even exist, but one of them – a lean, tall blond senior – moved aside politely to let her pass.

'But come *on*, dude,' one of the others said. 'If you really want to get air, you have to –'

Spreading out his arms, he leaped up, miming skateboarding as his friends applauded. The blond boy shook his head, grinning.

'No way, bro. Watch and learn. If you want the best way to get air –'

. . . *Try breathing in, then out?* Olivia thought wryly. She opened her mouth to make the joke.

Then she saw the intent looks on all the boys' faces, and sighed. She didn't think any of them would find it funny. As the blond launched into his own high-leaping mime, she turned to the line of lockers, squinting to find her own locker number among all the black paint. As soon as she spotted it, she started working on the combination lock. What was the code again? *Three . . . forty-nine . . .*

'That's it!' a voice bellowed behind her. Olivia spun around, her breath catching.

A sour-faced teacher in a stiff grey jacket was charging towards the skater-boys, clearing the hallway in his wake. 'Get off that skateboard *this minute*, Finn Jorgensen! What have I told you about skating indoors?'

Olivia had to leap out of his way, bumping

hard into her new locker. The teacher was so intent on his prey, though, he didn't even notice.

Finn, Olivia thought. Wasn't that the name of the skater-boy Sophia had been crushing on? It had to be the tall blond boy in the centre of the group. The teacher was heading straight for him.

'This time you'll have detention for . . . for . . . uh . . .' The teacher stuttered to a halt as he finally reached Finn – whose feet were planted solidly on the ground. There wasn't a single skateboard in sight. 'Where did it go?'

'No worries, Mr Russell,' Finn said. Shrugging, he stepped back and pointed to the wall of lockers, where a bright blue-and-red skateboard stood safely propped. 'See?' he said calmly. 'Everything's just like it's supposed to be. I wouldn't break the rules.'

'Well . . .' Mr Russell's face reddened. He pulled at his necktie, nearly choking himself.

'See that you don't!' He glowered around the group of boys, patting his collar back into place. 'I'll be watching you. *All* of you!'

With a huff, he spun on one heel and marched off.

Whew, Olivia thought. She let out the breath she'd been holding as she'd hidden by the locker. *I've never had a teacher go after me like that!*

Finn's friends were obviously fuming. 'What a jerk,' the closest boy muttered, glaring after the teacher. 'He needs a life of his own. Or someone to teach him a lesson.'

Finn was laughing, though, and shaking his head. 'Poor old Mr *Fuss*ell,' he said. 'Come on, guys. I feel bad for him. He's always so disappointed when he can't get us in trouble.'

'But what is *wrong* with him, man?' Another of Finn's friends shook his head. 'Do you think he's some kind of secret agent for the goth crowd?'

As Olivia rolled her eyes and turned back to her locker, she heard the other skaters chiming in enthusiastically.

'I bet he is!'

'Those goths are always out to get us.'

'I hate them!'

'Oh . . .' Finn's voice was a low mumble. 'Y'know, not *all* goths are bad . . .'

Really? Halfway through unloading her bag, Olivia looked up in surprise. This school seemed so divided, it was a pleasure to hear someone talking nicely about another group.

Then she glanced at Finn and realised he wasn't even looking at his friends. Instead, he was gazing over their heads at . . .

Amelia. The grim Goth-Queen stood surrounded by a group of other goth-girls who might as well have called themselves an Amelia tribute band. Every one of them was dressed like an Amelia-clone in identical black leather jackets and matching earrings, and they clustered around her with adoring expressions.

Amelia wasn't looking at any of them, though. She was looking straight at Finn . . . and for just a moment, Olivia glimpsed a slight smile playing at Amelia's black-painted lips.

I wonder if it hurts her face? Olivia thought. *It has to be rare that anything cracks that grim expression!*

A moment later, Amelia had converted the smile into a scowl . . . but it wasn't entirely convincing. She might have been trying to look hostile towards Finn, but instead she just looked uncomfortable . . . like there was a stone in her shoe. *Or a boy she can't make herself dislike!*

Whoa. Olivia felt as if her own eyeballs were bouncing back and forth like tennis balls over a net as she looked from one to the other and back again. Even now that Amelia had managed to force a scowl, she and Finn were *still* staring at each other. It was as if they *couldn't* look away.

There is some serious crushing going on, Olivia thought. *Between the leaders of the two groups who seem to hate each other the most!*

Finally, Finn's glance dropped to the floor, and his shoulders sagged. He laughed, obviously trying to fit back in to his friends' conversation. 'Funny,' he said.

But Olivia was pretty sure none of his friends had actually made a joke.

As the crowd of skater-boys filed down the hall on their way to class, the goth-girls all pointedly looked away . . . except for Amelia. She'd angled her head so that her fringe fell over her eyes, but she was surreptitiously watching Finn through the veil of hair.

And when he didn't return her gaze, the look of disappointment on Amelia's face made

Olivia's heart hurt.

Brrrrring!

The school bell sounded, and Olivia jumped. She'd spent so much time watching the action around her, she'd barely even started preparing for class! Hastily, she tipped her notebooks for that afternoon's classes into her locker, scooped up her bag and her school map, and slammed her locker door shut. *I'll have to wait until later to add some pictures and colour to the inside of the door!*

As she hurried towards her homeroom, though, she felt a fizz of excitement in her stomach, replacing all the nerves that she'd felt earlier.

I love a romance, she thought happily.

Her own romance might have to stay long-distance, at least for now . . . but she couldn't imagine anything more fun than helping another couple get together while she waited to see Jackson again. Matchmaking was one of her favourite activities – and that was lucky for Finn and Amelia, because they obviously needed help! This school was so divided between goth and mainstream, how could Finn and Amelia ever openly declare their feelings for each other without a helpful nudge?

Even as she thought that, she heard Ivy's exasperated voice in her head: *'You can't tell how they really feel just from watching them for less than two minutes.'*

'Oh, yes, I can!' Olivia blurted out.

A pair of goths nearby gave her startled looks.

Oops. She hadn't meant to say that out loud!

'Is Ivy's twin *talking to herself*?' one of the goths whispered loudly.

The other shook his head sadly. 'I guess not everyone in her family is cool.'

Whatever. Olivia ignored them. She had bigger things to worry about . . . like figuring out how to bring down the social barriers of Franklin Grove High!

Matchmaking Amelia and Finn wouldn't just make the two of them happy – it would bring all the school's barriers crashing down.

And I'm just the person to make it happen. Olivia gave a decisive nod as she stepped into her classroom.

If she'd needed any more proof of how much this school needed help, it was right here in homeroom, where the social groups were so clearly laid out, they might as well have put up signs and gateposts by each set of desks.

The goth-crowd owned the 'primo' tables, sitting by the window towards the back of the class. Meanwhile, the bunnies were stuck all the way in front, completely unable to join any of the 'cool' conversations because they would have to turn around in their desks.

Olivia shook her head, sighing, and looked for Ivy. *I might have known.*

Ivy was boxed in right in the far corner of the room, besieged by goths. As they pressed around her, Olivia saw her eyes fill with more and more panic and frustration until she looked like a trapped tiger.

'. . . But is that show *really* cool, Ivy? I mean, I know everyone says it is, but what do *you* think? If *you* tell me, I'll know what's right.'

'Do *you* think the Pall Bearers sold out with their latest album? I mean, they used *keyboards* – that's the opposite of goth! Isn't it?'

Uh-oh, Olivia thought. She could see an ultimate death-squint ready to form on her sister's face. *No one* trash-talked the Pall Bearers in front of Ivy and survived!

'Hey, Olivia.' It was Sophia, sitting in the exact centre of the classroom in a spot neither popular nor outcast. She smiled ruefully and patted the empty desk beside her. 'There's no point trying to fight your way through Ivy's flock of bats.'

Olivia sank down into her seat, still watching her twin. 'Do you think we should intervene?'

Sophia sighed. 'There's nothing we can do. Trust me – I've tried.'

The goths' voices grew louder and louder as they all competed for Ivy's attention. 'But Ivy –'

'Ivy –'

'Ivy –'

'Hey!' Ivy suddenly surged out of her seat. 'I need some thinking time!'

'Thinking time?' The closest goth-girl shook her head while all the others gasped. 'What's that?'

'I just . . .' Ivy sank back down into her seat, looking defeated. 'I want to . . . meditate,' she mumbled. 'I need to . . . find my chin.'

'Um . . .?' One of the other girls hesitantly

pointed to Ivy's face. 'Isn't it right there?'

Olivia had to choke down her laugh. None of the others might understand, but Ivy was definitely quoting Olivia's adoptive father . . . only she had gotten the quote a little bit wrong. Olivia was pretty sure she'd meant to say 'Jee'.

Unless it was 'Chi'? She'd never been sure.

'Whatever,' Ivy muttered. 'I just . . . I need to have my own headspace before school really starts.'

'Oh, yes.'

'*So* smart.'

'I *always* do that too, Ivy!'

The other goths all fluttered back to their own desks.

'Mondays are *intense*!' the closest goth-boy said solemnly.

Then they all folded their hands and closed their eyes.

Ivy looked around the intently meditating

group and shook her head, looking desperate. Then she put on her headphones and closed her eyes, slumping down in her seat.

'Look!' One of the goths had snuck one eye open to peek, and now they nudged another one, pointing to Ivy. 'She even meditates better than anybody!'

Little do they know, Olivia thought, *Ivy isn't meditating on anything . . . except maybe on how much she hates being popular!*

She sighed as she turned back to Sophia. 'This can't go on.'

'What can we do?' Sophia shrugged. 'They love her.'

'But you can see the pressure getting to her already,' Olivia said. *Just like it did at Wallachia Academy in Transylvania*, she realised. The memory made her shoulders stiffen.

Olivia hadn't been able to help her sister at that

snooty school for vampires, but she was here for Ivy now . . . and she wouldn't let her twin down.

She looked around the room and shook her head. 'There are so many social walls built around everyone at this high school, it's unbelievable.'

'Tell me about it,' Sophia groaned. 'I've never seen anything like this before.'

'Then let's do something about it!' Olivia nodded decisively. 'These walls need breaking down . . . and I'm the one with the sledgehammer!'

'You?' Sophia gave a snort of laughter as she looked up and down Olivia's glittering pink top, flippy skirt and sequinned bag. 'Olivia Abbott with a sledgehammer – now, that would *really* be unbelievable!'

Chapter Three

Ivy took a deep breath as she joined the lunch line in cafeteria. *I can do this. Of course I can. It's not a big deal.*

It was ridiculous to get annoyed by people liking her. Wasn't it?

So why do I feel like yelling?

All around her was a sea of *eyes* that seemed to follow her wherever she went, even as she stood waiting for the lunch ladies to pass her a plate of food. The feeling of being watched made the skin between her shoulder blades itch with discomfort. *I don't get it! Why is everybody acting this way?*

There was no good reason for all this worship. She was just a normal girl! . . . *Well, normal by Franklin Grove standards, anyway*, Ivy thought ruefully. But honestly, it wasn't as if the kids here knew anything really special about her. Back in Transylvania, Ivy was kind-of-sort-of-royalty, and all the other kids at Wallachia Academy had known it, but here she was just another goth.

Just imagine if anyone else at this school knew I was royal! She shuddered at the thought. *Oh, my darkness. That would be my worst nightmare!*

As soon as she'd paid for her lunch, she turned around – and saw heads drop as bunny students desperately tried to pretend they hadn't been watching her. Ivy had to stifle a scream of pure frustration.

Seriously, people. I am not that cool!

Was it time for desperate measures? As she walked towards a table in the corner of the room, she desperately tried to think of new ideas. *Maybe I could drop my tray?* If everyone saw her act like an embarrassing klutz, that would have to undo her popularity . . . wouldn't it?

But then I wouldn't have anything to eat! Her stomach growled in protest at the idea. After a morning spent under relentless social attack, she was starving. No way could she give up her lunch, even if it was only a measly medium burger!

As she passed a table full of goths, one hopeful-looking girl piped up, 'Here, Ivy! You can sit with us if you want.'

She started to push out a chair just as Ivy passed – and the chair smashed *hard* into Ivy's leg.

The girl's face went sickly green with horror. Gasps filled the air as the entire cafeteria turned to stare.

Argh. Ivy stifled a groan. *I don't have time for this!*

The truth was, she'd felt no pain at all. With

vampiric RHP on her side, the hit had felt like only a light tap. But from the way the chair had crashed into her, it obviously would have hurt a *human*.

So Ivy had no choice . . .

'Ohhh . . .' She bent over, grimacing as if in agony. Acting with all her might, she rubbed at her leg through her long black skirt.

'I am so, so sorry!' The goth-girl was almost crying now, her voice choked. 'I *never* meant to hurt you.'

'Don't worry about it,' Ivy muttered. '*Really.*'

Even as she spoke, her vampire hearing picked up the conversations erupting all over the cafeteria.

'Did you see that?'

'Oh, she's so grounded, even when she's in pain!'

'She even looks cool when she winces!'

Oh, my darkness. Ivy rolled her eyes. *Are they seriously idolising the way I look when I'm 'in pain'? They're going to love me in math class!*

As she straightened, the goth-girl jumped up, grabbing Ivy's arm in a desperate grip. 'I'm just *so* sorry. I'm Bela, by the way. Let me make it up to you? My father has a store card at Macy's. *Please* let me take you there this afternoon! You can pick up a gift and –'

'No! No, thank you.' Ivy yanked her hand out of Bela's clinging grip. *Too. Much. Apologising!*

Bela looked crushed.

Ivy bit her tongue against the death-squint she could feel forming on her face. Then she winced at the sudden stab of pain. *I really need to get to the dentist, and soon!*

Through gritted teeth, she said, 'It's fine. *I'm* fine. But, Bela, please. Get. Out. Of. My. Way.'

By the time she finally got to the corner table

she'd been aiming for, she felt like she'd been through a battlefield. She looked down at her medium burger and groaned. *It has to be cold by now.*

Then again . . . *Silver lining? Maybe it'll do a good impression of a real, rare burger!*

Quirking her lips at the idea, she sat down. Immediately, she realised her tactical mistake. *Uh-oh.*

The small, rectangular table she'd chosen could seat up to six people. All five empty seats were just waiting to be filled . . . and, based on recent events, people were going to want to sit *with* her now! She could already feel the eyes on her from the rest of the cafeteria, and hear the furious whispering as people debated whether or not they dared to join her.

Don't even think about it! Ivy hunched her shoulders defensively, leaning over her tray. She'd promised Olivia they would sit together at lunch.

Not only did she want to spend more time with her sister, but she really wanted all the other students to get used to her having a non-goth twin. Then maybe they'd stop whispering rude things about her . . . and Ivy would stop wanting to punch them all!

Unfortunately, Olivia's first stop at lunchtime had to be the school counsellor's office, to work out her late-enrolment issues. She wouldn't be here for at least ten minutes.

How am I supposed to guard five empty seats for that whole time, all by myself?

Clenching her hands around her burger, she sent off her strongest *Don't come near me* vibes and bit into the burger, hard.

The burger was every bit as cold as she'd imagined. Tough, chewy and flavourless. She forced herself to keep eating just to fill her stomach, but it couldn't hold her attention as she felt the cafeteria filling up around her. *Come on, Olivia. Hurry up!*

Tapping one booted foot nervously under the table, Ivy mentally counted off the number of spare seats against the number of students and trays. Soon, she might have no choice but to let someone sit opposite her . . . and no matter how hard she tried, she couldn't think of any way to translate 'Get away from me' into polite English. *There's only so much grumpiness the word 'please' can excuse!*

She closed her eyes for a moment in despair. *Oh, my darkness, it's only the second week of school. What will I be like by the end of the year?*

As she chewed doggedly on her unappealing burger, taking tiny bites to minimise the taste, a parade of people tried to 'subtly' walk by her with their trays of food, their footsteps lagging as they passed her table. She tried not to look, but she couldn't miss the way their eyes lit up with hope – hope that she might let them sit at her table.

Argh. Ivy couldn't bear it. *How do I reject them without being mean?*

She lunged for her bag, searching for something she could use as a shield. Textbooks wouldn't work, but maybe . . . *Yes!* She could feel a small paperback inside. *Maybe if I'm totally absorbed in reading, people will leave me alone!*

She snatched the paperback out of her bag and opened it to the middle section, as if she were already halfway through. Almost burying her face in it, she began to fake-read without even looking at the cover, screwing up her face in an expression of intense concentration.

Behind her, she heard someone gasp. Then someone else whispered, 'Is she really reading . . . *that*?'

'I can't believe it,' another girl murmured.

'Of all the people I never thought would read that book –'

Um . . .? Ivy blinked and switched from fake-reading to real-reading.

'He clasped her in an embrace so tight, she could not escape . . . nor did she want to. She would be his prisoner of love . . . forever!'

Ivy stifled a groan. *Oh, no.*

She knew that awful writing style and that unintentionally funny romance vibe. This was *Bare Throats at Sunset* by S. K. Reardon! Ivy had become friends with his daughter Holly this summer, but she'd been outraged by the way the book presented vampires. Still, Lillian had insisted that Ivy should give it another try, claiming it was the ultimate guilty pleasure. Ivy had finally stuck it in her bag last week just to make her stepmom happy. She'd planned to read it when no one was looking.

Now *everyone* was looking – and she'd practically plastered her face to the pages in her attempt to keep people away from her. She must have looked as if she were *loving* it!

Ivy's face burned. *Everyone's going to think I have the worst taste ever!*

. . . *Hey, wait!* A sudden flutter of hope sparked inside her. *If they think I actually enjoy this book, maybe they'll stop thinking I'm cool. Maybe they'll realise I'm actually just . . . uh . . . warm?*

But the next conversation she heard destroyed her hope.

'Wow . . . Maybe that book isn't so bad, after all.'

'If *Ivy* likes it . . .'

'I'm going to get a copy, too.'

'Maybe we should re-evaluate S.K. Reardon. He may have made a serious contribution to literature.'

I can't believe this! Ivy slammed down the book

on the table, fighting the impulse to scream.

'Or maybe not,' another girl whispered. 'I think she's turned against it.'

Ivy closed her eyes and counted to ten. When she finally thought she could hold herself back, she opened her eyes again and reached for her burger. Just as her fingers touched it, she stilled. *Wait a minute. Maybe it's not too late to prove that I'm un-cool.*

What if she ate messily – and not just a *little* messily, but horribly, sloppily, like a pig? Then the other kids would *have* to stop mooning over her!

It's worth a try. Steeling herself, she grabbed her burger and took a huge, messy bite. Ketchup exploded over her chin and cheeks, through the air, on to the table . . .

. . . and just as she smeared it across her face, she looked up to find her boyfriend staring down at her in disbelief.

Oh, no!

Ivy wanted to disappear.

Brendan's eyes widened as his gaze went from her ketchup-smeared face to the ketchup she had sprayed across the table.

It's OK, Ivy told herself, trying to slow her suddenly rocketing heart-rate. *We've been together for a long time. He knows this isn't really me. Right?*

As she sat frozen, unable to speak, Brendan's lips twitched. Then he began to laugh.

'Uh . . . you want one of these, maybe?' Still laughing, he handed her a paper napkin from the dispenser on the table. 'You look just like a movie vampire!'

Rolling her eyes, Ivy snatched the napkin from his hands and hastily wiped off her face. '*Movie* vampire, huh?' She gave him a mock-snarl.

Brendan recoiled, his laughter dying. 'Whoa.' His voice dropped to a concerned whisper.

'Your teeth *really* need filing.'

'I know, I know.' Ivy winced. 'I'm going to the dentist soon, I promise. But first, you need to sit down *fast*.'

'Really?' He looked around the nearly-empty table, shaking his head. 'Have you been saving *all* the seats just for me?'

'Doofus.' She groaned, trying to ignore the ripple of excitement and gossip that passed around the room as Brendan sat down beside her.

It was impossible to ignore the squeals that rose from the very next table, though. 'O.M.G.!' one girl gasped. 'Do you think Ivy has a *boyfriend*?'

'I can't take this much longer,' Ivy muttered under her breath. 'I'm not cut out for popularity! I feel like I have to perform, or something – and I am *not* the actress in the family.'

Brendan rubbed her back in warm, comforting circles. 'I know.'

'Ooh,' another girl at the next table sighed. 'They look *serious*.'

Ivy winced. 'Do you think it'll ever get better?' She eased into his touch, starting to relax. 'Once people get used to me, they'll see I'm not so special, and everything will calm down . . . right?'

Brendan shrugged. 'Maybe I'm not the person to ask.' His dark hair flopped over his eyes as he leaned towards her, smiling. 'From the moment I realised you were the coolest girl in the world, I've been realising it every day, over and over again.'

Ivy tried to fight it, but she couldn't stop a grin invading her face. 'You big sap!'

Then she bit back a curse as she realised her mistake. How could she have been so dumb? She'd smiled. And smiling made her look friendly.

Big, big mistake!

It was too late to take it back. Goth-girls from

her grade were suddenly swarming the table, beaming at her hopefully.

Don't panic, Ivy told herself. *There are only four of them*. But that didn't lessen the feeling of an attack as they all swooped at once, filling every empty chair. *See, this is why smiling is stupid*, she lectured herself. *It lands you in uncomfortable situations!*

'So . . . how *exactly* do you two know each other?' the first goth-girl drawled. 'Hmm?'

The other three leaned in to listen, setting their chins on their hands and staring at Brendan with open curiosity.

'You can tell *us*,' the second girl purred. 'Is it serious?'

'Ivy deserves the *best*, you know,' the third girl said pointedly.

Ivy stiffened with outrage even as Brendan gave a tiny, meaningful shake of his head, telling her without words not to worry about it.

I am not going to sit here and let him be insulted! Ivy opened her mouth to tell the other girls *exactly* how important Brendan was to her . . .

. . . then stopped herself with a jerk. *Wait a minute. The last thing I need to do is to make romantic declarations 'cool'!*

She was still trying to figure out how to respond when she heard a familiar voice behind her. 'Uhm . . . ?'

Oh, no. Ivy looked up, and her stomach did a backflip. It was Olivia, tray in hand, standing behind her . . . and looking at the completely-full table, without a single space available.

'Olivia . . .' Ivy began. She twisted around, looking for another chair to pull up to the table.

'I don't think there's any space left,' the first goth-girl said coolly.

'Yeah,' said the third goth-girl. 'What a *pity*.'

Just explain it to them simply – this doesn't have to be

anything dramatic. Ivy gritted her teeth, starting a count to ten in her head . . .

Only to find Olivia backing away from her.

'Don't worry about it.' Olivia gave her a bright, tight smile. To anyone but Ivy, she would have looked completely unbothered . . . but Ivy knew her twin. 'I'll catch up with you later,' Olivia said breezily.

Ivy shook her head, glimpsing the hurt hidden behind Olivia's expression. 'But –'

It was too late. Olivia had already spun around and hurried away, her pink shoes clicking against the cafeteria floor. A moment later, she'd disappeared into the crowd of strangers, by herself.

Ripples of reaction ran through the cafeteria, and Ivy's vampire ears forced every whisper on her.

'Did you see that? Even her own *twin* isn't cool enough to sit with her!'

'Of course not.' Someone let out a snort of disgust. 'Just look at all that pink!'

Fury tightened every muscle in Ivy's body. Under the table, Brendan took her hand and gave it a comforting squeeze. He was the only person who could know exactly what she'd just heard . . . and how hard it was for her not to react.

Ivy squeezed his hand back, grateful for his support . . . but it wasn't enough. *This can never happen again.* OK, she couldn't find Olivia a place at her table *this* lunch hour, but she could do her best to fix things.

Starting now!

Squaring her shoulders, she looked at the goth-girl directly across the table from her, who was wearing a *Shadowtown* T-shirt.

The truth was, *Shadowtown* was Ivy's favourite show . . . but it was undeniably trashy. And so far, no one else at Franklin Grove High knew about

Ivy's midnight marathons of *Shadowtown*. So . . .

She forced her face into a sneer. 'So, is *that* how you like your vampires?' She pointed dismissively at the other girl's T-shirt. 'Moon-eyed and sappy?'

'Uh . . .' Brendan stared at her, visibly shocked. 'Ivy –'

She gave him a gentle kick under the table. The last thing she wanted right now was for him to blurt out how much Ivy loved *Shadowtown* and its sappy, moon-eyed vampires.

Brendan closed his mouth obediently, but his eyes were wide as she continued, 'I mean, don't you think all of that –' She waved her hand in the general direction of the *Shadowtown* T-shirt, forcing poison into her tone –'is a bit *pathetic*?'

The girl rocked backwards as if she'd been punched . . . and Ivy's stomach gave a sickening twist.

The whole table had fallen silent with shock.

Everyone for three tables around was watching Ivy and her victim, waiting to see what would happen next.

It's for the best, Ivy told herself, fighting down guilt. Really, this whole horrible scene was for the poor girl's own good, and everyone else's, too. If they all decided Ivy was horrible, they wouldn't want anything more to do with her. Then they'd all find something more interesting to do with their lives – and she'd finally be left in peace to settle in at her new school without everyone analysing her every move.

Still, she couldn't stand the look of hurt in the other girl's eyes. Crossing her arms, she looked pointedly away, studying the rest of the cafeteria. As her gaze picked out Olivia in the crowd, she let out a sigh of relief. Thank goodness, her twin hadn't ended up stuck at a table full of strangers – Sophia had made space for her at the skater table with Finn and his friends. Between Olivia's pink top, Sophia's black dress and the rest of the skaters' tie-dyed or gingham outfits, they looked like an odd mixture of students to be sitting together . . . and that was exactly how it should be.

Ivy was just wishing that she could be part of it when she suddenly heard a piercing gasp. She swung back around to her own table and found *Shadowtown* Girl staring down at her T-shirt. When the goth-girl straightened, she was beaming with delight. 'I get it! You're quoting from that scene in series two, episode four, aren't you?'

Uh-oh. Ivy swallowed hard. Was she? She hadn't *thought* she was . . . but now that Laura pointed it out . . .

'When that vampire guy makes fun of the sweater his girlfriend is wearing,' Laura went on 'to try to make her dump him because he knows he's not good enough for her! But she doesn't, she just loves him even more because she can see through his act and knows he's a good person underneath.' Her eyes misting, the girl reached across the table and grabbed Ivy's hand. 'I can't believe this. I've *never* met anyone who knows *Shadowtown* as well as I do. You are the *coolest*!'

As all the other goth-girls around the table chimed in with agreement, Ivy sagged in despair.

So much for that plan! She'd just accidentally made herself more popular than ever!

When she looked at Brendan, she found his cheeks sucked in tight to try to hide his smile . . . but she could tell he was laughing on the inside, even while she was dying.

And it was still only Monday!

Chapter Four

'I just miss you,' Olivia whispered into the phone that evening, as she sat curled up on her bed.

'I miss you, too.' Her boyfriend's voice was warm and confident, and just the sound of it made her shoulders relax. 'But things will get easier at school soon. I know it. Hey, you're a movie star now, remember?'

Olivia rolled her eyes, but she couldn't help laughing as she propped herself up against her pale lavender pillows. 'Yeah, maybe I should tell the goths at school to keep that in mind.'

Jackson laughed too, but when he spoke again, his tone was serious. 'Just remember, it could be a lot worse. You wouldn't want to be fighting off paparazzi every day, right? That's why you went back to Franklin Grove in the first place – because you wanted a normal life. No Hollywood lifestyle, no hangers-on . . .'

'You're right.' Olivia took a deep breath. 'Of course you're right. And if that means being unpopular . . . that's OK.' She nodded firmly, bracing herself. 'I don't need to be popular to be happy.'

The doorbell rang downstairs, and she jumped up, balancing the phone against her ear. 'Oh, Camilla's here! I've got to go.'

'Have fun tonight,' Jackson said, 'and say hi to her for me, OK?'

'I will.' Beaming, Olivia hung up and hurried down the stairs to the front door, where her best friend was waiting.

Olivia hadn't seen Camilla since she'd left for filming. Now that high school had started, they weren't even going to the same school any more . . . but they had vowed to hold sleepovers every two weeks to make up for it. Even though it was a school night, their parents had allowed them to hold their first sleepover, on the absolute promise that they would go to bed on time.

Just the sight of Camilla's grinning face under her big glasses and floppy new velvet beret was enough to make Olivia start to feel like she was really home again, after all the weirdness of the filming, the jet lag and her bizarre new school. And as they went into the kitchen to make potato salad for dinner, Camilla's burbling energy was infectious.

'I missed you so much!' Camilla bounced into a movie director's pose, holding out her hands to frame Olivia's face as if she were directing a shot. 'Scene: A school hallway . . . but something is missing from the picture!' She dropped her hands, sighing. 'School is so different without you.'

'I know.' Olivia winced as she thought of just how different her new school was. Shaking it aside, she leaned over to pull out a sack of potatoes from a storage drawer.

'I mean, Charlotte Brown is great, of course!' Camilla said. 'But it's not the same.'

'Excuse me?' Olivia jerked upright, the sack of potatoes slipping out of her hands. 'Did you just say Charlotte Brown was *great*?' She stared at Camilla. 'Are we talking about the same Charlotte Brown?'

As the queen bee of Franklin Grove Middle School, Charlotte had tormented them relentlessly all through eighth grade.

'Well . . .' Camilla shrugged and picked up a

carrot stick from the platter Mrs Abbott had left on the counter earlier that evening. 'She's changed. She's actually really fun to be around, now. She's good at organising events, and we're working together on the school play.'

'Wow.' Olivia shook her head in wonder as Camilla crunched the carrot stick. 'So . . . you and *Charlotte Brown* are BFFs now?'

Camilla cringed, almost dropping the carrot. 'No! Not exactly. More like . . . maybe SOFFNs?'

Olivia laughed helplessly. *And Ivy thought film language was hard to understand!* 'What does that even mean?' she asked, as she leaned back over to pick up the potatoes.

'I just made it up.' Camilla grinned, looking delighted with herself. 'Do you like it? It means Sort-of-Friends-For-Now.'

'Got it.' Olivia smiled ruefully. 'No long-term commitment.'

'We'll just have to see how it goes,' Camilla said. Her brows lowered as she finished the carrot stick. 'Have you noticed how high school changes people?'

Olivia sighed. 'That is *very* true.'

The last thing she wanted to think about right now was how much everyone seemed to have changed . . . even her own twin. So she was only too glad when Camilla launched into questions about the filming experience on the set of *Eternal Sunset*. Olivia might not know all the technical details that Camilla, a director herself, was curious about, but thinking about the London shoot was a perfect distraction from the day she'd had.

Camilla looked out through the kitchen window. Olivia saw her notice Mr Abbott standing silently with his back to them, his hands together and his head slightly bowed.

Camilla's eyes widened, and she stopped in the

middle of a question about film cameras. 'Um . . . is your dad praying?'

'Oh, no. He's *meditating.*' Olivia frowned, putting down the potato she was peeling as she tried to remember what he'd told her earlier. 'He's looking for some kind of energy, but I can't quite remember what it is. "Jee" energy, maybe? Or "T" energy . . . or maybe even "B" energy! It could be any of them . . . but definitely not "Chin"!'

Sudden laughter burbled out of her as she remembered Ivy's desperate attempt in homeroom. *I wonder if she's found her chin yet?*

Olivia was pretty sure she'd seen the real word Ivy was trying for on one of her dad's books once . . . but she thought it was spelled with a 'Q', not a 'Ch'!

'Ohh-kay.' Shrugging, Camilla started chopping potatoes as she launched back into her interrogation about the movie set.

After the third straight question about camera lenses, though, Olivia had to give up. 'I'm sorry! I'm really not all that familiar with the technical stuff. I was just focused on remembering my lines.'

'Oh.' Camilla slumped. 'And you didn't ask a single question about what frame-rates they were using?'

'Um, well . . . no.' Olivia winced at the disappointment on her friend's face. Turning away, she swept the potato peels into the compost. 'It just didn't occur to me. But it will next time, I promise!'

'We-e-ell . . .' Camilla gave a melodramatic sigh, then winked. 'I guess I can wait.' Hopefully, she added, 'When will the next time be, exactly?'

Olivia groaned, falling back against the kitchen counter. 'This weekend. Already! Can you believe it?' As her friend started to mix together the final ingredients in a large clay mixing bowl, Olivia said, 'It'll be another whole *week* of shooting. I told my teachers, and they've piled up so much homework for me to take, I don't know how I'll get through it all! When I open my mouth on set next week, I might just start reciting weird historical test questions instead of my character's lines.'

'Olivia Abbott, less than perfect on-screen?' Camilla smiled, setting down her spoon. 'It'll never happen. You know I'm right. Now, what else do you want for dinner, besides the potato salad?'

'Honestly?' Olivia shrugged. 'I'm feeling in the mood for cereal!'

Camilla blinked. 'Are you joking?'

'I wish,' Olivia said. 'I'm still so jet-lagged, my body seems to think it's morning! In fact – I'm so jet-lagged, I even thought that . . . oh, never mind.' She slumped.

'What?' Camilla frowned.

'Nothing,' Olivia said. 'It's dumb. I just . . . I shouldn't talk about this.' She turned away and pulled down a box of cereal. 'Let's eat now, OK?'

'No, tell me.' Camilla put one hand on her arm. 'What is it?'

'It's . . .' Olivia bit her lip. 'There was just a weird moment at lunch today . . . well . . . Ivy didn't *want* me to sit with her,' she finished in a rush.

'What?' Camilla stared at her. 'That doesn't sound like Ivy.'

Olivia shrugged unhappily. 'Honestly, at the time I was just confused. But now that I've had time to think about it . . . well, it's kind of getting to me.' As hurt bubbled up inside her, she had to take a deep breath, focusing on pouring her cereal without spilling it. 'She promised we'd sit together at lunch, but when I got there, the whole table was filled with goths. There wasn't a single space left. And . . . well, the goths at that school *hate* people like me.'

Camilla shook her head as she took down a box of cereal for herself. 'Do you seriously think Ivy would snub you just to please someone else?'

'No!' Olivia said. 'Of course not. But . . .' Her voice lowered to a whisper. 'When another girl snubbed me, Ivy didn't say a word. The truth is, I'm worried about her. I think she's not finding it so easy to be herself.'

Or easy to stand up for what she believes in. Olivia sighed.

Where was her twin tonight? At home, hiding? Or out with one of her new friends . . . the ones who sneered at everything pink?

'Well . . .' Camilla blinked, giving a quick headshake as her gaze passed over Mr Abbott in the garden. 'Wow, he still hasn't moved. What martial art is he practising, Statue-Do?'

Olivia smiled weakly. 'Maybe.'

'Never mind.' Camilla turned back to Olivia, a determined look in her eye. 'Look, I strongly, *strongly* doubt that Ivy didn't want to be seen with you. High school is a weird time for everyone, you know? It was probably just a misunderstanding.'

'Yeah.' Olivia sighed. 'At least it wasn't all bad.' Her lips twitched into a mischievous smile. 'I actually ended up sitting with a group of senior boys!'

'Oh, reeaally?' Camilla drawled. Putting on a mock-stern look, she added, 'And what would your *boyfriend* have to say about that?'

'Oh, shut up!' Giggling, Olivia shoved her playfully. 'I didn't mean it like *that*. But I wanted to get a better read on one of them, anyway.

His name's Finn, and –'

'Finn, hmm?' Camilla waggled her eyebrows as she poured her own cereal. 'I bet he has blond hair. Am I right?'

'Of course you are.' Olivia carried the big bowl of potato salad to the table, with two sets of forks and spoons stuck inside, and Camilla followed with the bowls of cereal. As the two girls settled in comfortably, Olivia explained the Finn-and-Amelia problem to her friend.

'So it's a *Romeo and Juliet* meets *West Side Story* vibe.' Camilla nodded knowledgeably as she scooped up a spoonful of potato salad. 'I've got it. We're talking romantic tragedy here.'

'I hope not!' Olivia shivered. 'Honestly, at first I was only interested because of that situation, but then I got a chance to actually talk to Finn at lunch – and he is kind of sweet! He coaches Lincoln Vale middle school kids in skateboarding every weekend. He's just a really nice guy . . . and, you know, I'm not so crazy about Amelia, but at least she's no Jessica Phelps.'

Camilla made a face. 'Ugh. The world does *not* need another Jessica Phelps!'

They both shuddered at the reminder of the awful Hollywood mega-star who'd schemed and stolen the lead role in *The Groves* from Olivia, then done her best to steal Olivia's *Eternal Sunset* role, too.

'Amelia's not so bad, though,' Olivia said firmly. 'I think if she had someone like Finn to balance her out, she might even be nice. So now I *really* want them to get together!'

'You do, huh?' Camilla looked at her thoughtfully. 'Tell me the truth, Olivia Abbott. Is this just because of what happened with Ivy at lunch?'

'No!' Olivia felt her cheeks heat up. 'Of course

not. But . . .' She ducked her head over her cereal as she admitted, 'I don't think I can deal with going to a school where I never get to have lunch with my own twin.'

'Hmm.' Camilla took a first, testing spoonful of cold cereal . . . and made a disgusted face. 'Yuck! I can't believe you eat this for fun.'

Olivia rolled her eyes. 'Not all of us eat French croissants for breakfast every day, Madam Director.'

'Whatever.' Camilla shoved the cereal bowl to one side. 'Here's the real point. You've been at high school for just *one day*, and you already have a bunch of homework. Do you really want to add to your boatload of stress by trying to match-make two people you've only just met?'

Olivia sat back. 'Why not? If it'll make life better for everyone –'

'Trust me,' said Camilla, 'every time people

meddle in romance in the movies, it *always* goes wrong and creates chaos.'

'But I really think I'm on to something here!' Olivia held up her two spoons to make a point, ignoring the milk and potato salad dripping from them. 'See, this is Finn and this is Amelia.' She wobbled the two spoons meaningfully. 'They want to move forwards, but they can't. The social divisions in the school are too defined. Without some help, they're going to be stuck in Act One forever.'

Narrowing her eyes, she spoke in the secret language guaranteed to get Camilla on board: 'They need an *inciting incident* to propel them into Act Two . . . and we are just the directors to make it happen!'

'Hmm.' Camilla's own eyes narrowed. Then her lips curved into a beaming grin. 'But of course. How could I refuse when you begged me in film-speak?'

'I knew it.' Olivia beamed. 'I'm getting good at Camilla-ese, aren't I?'

'You're definitely learning. And maybe . . . maybe we *could* rewrite the script.' Camilla's eyes narrowed and her jaw pushed outwards into her *all-business* look as her fingers started tapping rapidly on the table. Olivia waited patiently as the wheels turned. Suddenly, Camilla's face lit up.

'Of course!' Camilla shook her head. 'How could I have been so blind? What the soon-to-be "Famelia" need is a good, old-fashioned "meet cute"!'

'I beg your pardon?' Olivia gave her friend a stern look. 'If you're going to be involved in this project, ma'am, our producers insist that you break up the Camilla-ese with a little bit of English from time to time!'

'I'll try.' Camilla giggled. 'But it's so perfect!

Can't you see? Movie romances almost always start by having the couple meet in a wacky way. It has to be a funny story they can tell their friends about later on – and then when things get rough in the second half of Act Two, one of them can always lament the *twist of fate* that brought them together. You know, "If only I hadn't walked into that police station . . ."'

'Have you gone a little bit wacky yourself?' Olivia stared at her, setting down her spoons. 'First of all, I do not see Finn and Amelia *ever* ending up in a police station. And secondly . . .' She shook her head. 'Why do things have to get rough?'

Camilla shrugged. 'Every romance needs a narrative obstacle, right?'

'No!' Olivia protested. 'Trust me. Jackson and I have had *more* than our fair share of those over the last year-and-a-bit, and they were *not* fun!

I wouldn't wish them on anybody.'

She shuddered at the memories . . . especially of that long, bleak period when they had actually broken up. *I never want to feel that way again!* She hung on to the memory of their latest phone call like a talisman. *Thank goodness we're back together.*

'Yeah, but you're reunited now, right?' Camilla raised her eyebrows. 'So it was all worth it, wasn't it?'

Olivia nodded. 'Totally.' As she finished her cereal, though, she thought hard. 'There's just one problem with your meet-cute plan,' she said. 'Finn and Amelia have *already* met . . . and no matter how that went down, it can't have been *that* adorable or wacky, because now they barely speak to each other. They don't even want anyone else to notice when they make eye contact!' Pushing aside her empty cereal bowl, she gave her friend a challenging look. 'What does Hollywood teach us about *this* situation?'

Camilla's eyes narrowed in concentration. 'What they need is to be *forced* into close proximity. They need to be put in a life or death situation that brings them together and forces them to face up to what is in their hearts! If they have no choice but to communicate, they'll eventually have to run out of topics other than their true feelings. Then –'

'Ahem.' Olivia cleared her throat. 'Did you just say *life or death*?' She raised her eyebrows at her friend. 'In *Franklin Grove*?'

Camilla burst into laughter. 'OK, OK! Well, maybe it doesn't have to be that extreme . . . but it has to be a situation that makes them both so uncomfortable that they start bonding. Something like . . . oh, I don't know –' she waved one hand in loose circles, obviously searching for inspiration – 'maybe they could be paired up on a science project together. I know – Chemistry!'

'Seriously?' Olivia groaned. 'That's the worst you can think of? You always had so much imagination! Maybe high school is changing you, too.'

'Well, I didn't mean it to be as boring as it sounds.' Camilla grimaced. 'But think about it: a sudden explosion is just the sort of dramatic, inciting incident to push an odd-couple relationship along!'

'I suppose . . .' Olivia sighed. 'But I want to get Finn and Amelia together, not singe off their eyebrows in a chem-experiment!'

Camilla shrugged. 'Detention, then? They can bond over their shared resentment of having to stay behind! *Oh*, yeah. Instead of thinking about how they broke a school rule –' She waggled her eyebrows meaningfully – 'they can think about how much they *looove* each other!'

Olivia stared at her. 'How long was I away in London? It can't have been long enough for you to undergo a full metamorphosis. Have you *always* been a Sappy Sally?'

Camilla rolled her eyes. 'This is for the good of the narrative, Olivia. That's *all* it's about.'

'Yeah, right.' Olivia poked her best friend in the shoulder, grinning. 'Come on, admit it. You're a secret romantic, aren't you?'

'Focus, Abbott!' Camilla shoved aside the potato salad bowl, looking as scary as a real film director. 'This is no time for jokes! We have a script to write. Now help me brainstorm while we make something *appropriate* for an evening meal.'

'Yes, ma'am!' Olivia gave a mock salute. 'Would sandwiches work?'

A faraway look came into Camilla's eyes. 'Hmm, sandwiches . . . Yes, those could work. Those could work *perfectly*!'

But it wasn't until they were standing at the chopping board with all the ingredients around them that Olivia figured out what her friend had had in mind.

'Right!' Camilla scooped up a hunk of cheese. 'So, here's Finn, and here's . . .' she picked up a lettuce leaf '. . . Amelia!'

'Really? As lettuce?' Olivia frowned. 'Amelia's a Goth-Queen. Remember?'

'Oh, all right, then.' Camilla dropped the lettuce and grabbed a black olive. 'Now, the chopping board is Franklin Grove High.' Rapidly, she laid out lettuce leaves to form corridors. All we have to do is figure out a way for Finn and Amelia to get detention!'

'Hmm.' Olivia bent in to help. 'Finn's easy to predict. That skateboard is bound to get him into trouble one day! Mr Russell's just bursting to give him detention for it.'

'Excellent!' Camilla gave the black olive a narrow-eyed look. 'And Amelia? What does our Goth-Queen do? Talk back to teachers? Scrawl graffiti on the walls?'

'No!' Olivia shook her head. 'Nothing like that. She may dress like a rebel – well, by the standards of most schools, anyway – but she's not a troublemaker.'

'No?' Camilla sagged with disappointment. 'Are you sure?'

'Positive.' Olivia grimaced. 'She's even getting top grades.'

'Drat.' Camilla sighed. 'How on earth are we going to get her into detention, then?'

As Olivia shook her head hopelessly, the kitchen door opened and Mr Abbott walked in, wearing his loose martial arts uniform. His eyes widened as he looked at the lettuce-maze the two girls had built on the chopping board.

'Ah . . . Olivia? Do you girls have some sort of a *scheme* going?'

'No, Dad!' Quickly, Olivia brushed the lettuce into a pile, obliterating the hallways of Franklin Grove High. 'It's just a . . . project. A project for school!'

Camilla nodded earnestly beside her . . . and really, Olivia told herself, she was telling the truth. It might not be official, but it was definitely a school-related project!

'I'm glad to hear it.' Mr Abbott smiled as he gave Olivia a pat on the shoulder. 'The *scheming* warrior will always be outfoxed by an *honest* one, you know.'

Olivia had to close her eyes so her dad wouldn't see them roll. 'Yes, Dad,' she said politely. In her head, though, she added: *But high school is hardly Warriorsville!*

'How did your meditation go, Mr Abbott?'

Camilla asked. 'Did you find your "T"?'

'That would be *Chi.* Spelled with a *Q.*' Mr Abbott sighed. 'But, alas . . . it remains elusive.'

Olivia opened her eyes and gave her dad a bracing smile. 'I'm sure you'll find it soon, Dad,' she said. 'And in the meantime . . .' She glanced at the chopping board full of ingredients. *How many people did we think we were cooking for?* 'Why don't you eat a nice sandwich to feel better?'

'Just don't eat that bit of cheese or black olive,' Camilla added, sweeping 'Finn' and 'Amelia' quickly out of the way. 'Because that would be really, really bad karma!'

Chapter Five

This is actually kind of awesome! Olivia thought the next afternoon, as she tailed Amelia through the hallways. The final bell had just rung to end the school day, and everyone was heading out . . . everyone except Olivia.

She'd never seen anything like the way the entire school created a path for Amelia as she moved. *Now, if only they would keep it open for me!* Unfortunately, the gap closed just behind Amelia, forcing Olivia to hop, skip and pirouette her way past the others to keep up with the Goth-Queen. She wondered if the ninth graders did the same for Ivy, and thought how weird she must find that experience. Yesterday, at lunch, Olivia had seen the indecision on Ivy's face, and knew that her twin was still having a tough time adjusting to high school. She had decided not to call Ivy last night, just in case talking about the whole thing made her twin feel even more pressured.

She had to run to finally catch up with Amelia, but at least there was one good side-effect: the breathlessness she had been planning to fake came completely naturally.

'A . . . A . . . Amelia!' she managed, panting.

'Yes?' Amelia raised her eyebrows, looking bored. 'Is something wrong?'

Aware of everyone around staring at them, Olivia drew on all of her acting exercises. *Remember: make eye contact! No stuttering! Minimal head movement!* Those were the rules that had helped her act convincingly on screen. Now she'd have to hope they helped her now.

'The principal is looking for you,' she said, looking straight into Amelia's eyes.

'Really?' Amelia frowned. 'Why wasn't there an announcement on the PA, then?'

'Uh . . .' Olivia paused. *No head movement,* she reminded herself, fighting to keep her head from ducking. *Keep eye contact!* 'I don't know,' she said. 'It's just . . . what I was told.'

As Amelia held her gaze, the Goth-Queen's eyes narrowed. Olivia forced herself to keep still. *This is why I hate lying!*

Finally, Amelia shrugged, sending silver chains clanking across her leather coat. 'Oh, fine. Like I didn't have enough to do today!' Growling, she turned on one heel. Just as she was starting to set off, though, she suddenly stopped, and sighed. 'Thank you,' she muttered. 'For telling me.'

'Er . . . no problem.' Olivia pasted a winning

smile on to her face. 'Happy to help.'

Rolling her eyes, Amelia turned away and stomped off down the hall.

Olivia waited a moment, then followed after her. She kept more of a distance this time, so that the Goth-Queen couldn't see her, ducking behind skateboarders and groups of goths whenever Amelia looked around. As she emerged from her latest hiding place, she found Ivy staring at her with raised eyebrows from across the hall.

What's going on? Ivy mouthed.

Olivia shrugged. She wished she could ask her twin for help . . . but Ivy was surrounded by her own cluster of goth groupies – all of whom were glaring contemptuously at Olivia now. There was no point trying to separate Ivy from them. Olivia had learned that much at lunch yesterday.

Shoving down the remembered hurt, she forced a smile. 'Tell you later!' she whispered.

It was a bare thread of sound, but she knew Ivy's vampire hearing would pick up on it.

Turning her back on her twin and the groupies, she hurried down the hallway. Amelia's black-leather coat had already disappeared from view, but Olivia slipped through the crowds and managed to lurk just outside the principal's office just a moment after Amelia had stalked inside.

She heard Amelia's annoyed voice. 'Is Mr Carson in?'

Score! Olivia did a high-jump in her head. Her plan had just been put into action! There was only one person sitting in the waiting room outside Mr Carson's office . . . so she knew exactly who Amelia must have spoken to, to ask that question.

Mr Fussell – *er, Russell*! – had erupted at Finn over lunch, as usual. Apparently, his skateboard wheels had come off and clattered on the ground when Finn had opened his locker, and Mr Russell had chased him all the way to the cafeteria to yell at him about it. Olivia had started out feeling sympathetic . . . but the moment Mr Russell had ordered Finn to go and see Principal Carson, Olivia's sympathy had turned into excitement. It was time to put the *Famelia* plan into motion!

Now she pressed her ears against the corner of the door just in time to hear Finn mumble: 'I think he's on the phone. He didn't answer when I knocked.'

Amelia snorted. 'And did you actually knock loud enough?'

There was a pause. Then Finn said, 'I may be *just* a simple skater, but I'm pretty sure even I can't mess up knocking on a door.'

'Hmm.' Amelia sounded unconvinced.

Olivia winced. *Why does she have to act so haughty with everyone? Can't she see how annoying it is?*

Amelia spoke again, her voice softer. 'I don't

think you're *just* a skater, you know.'

Whoa! Olivia jerked upright. *Progress! That was definite progress! Now just let Finn say . . . let him say . . .*

'Ughlflp!'

What? Olivia blinked, shaking her head.

Apparently Finn had been so taken by surprise, he'd lost the power of speech . . . because all that Olivia could hear were choking noises.

Smooth, Finn. Smooth. She muffled a groan as she heard the choking noises fade away, followed only by an awkward silence.

Still, the Skater King and the Goth-Queen were both trapped there for the moment, forced to sit next to each other with nothing else to do. Surely they *had* to start a real conversation soon?

But they didn't! Olivia couldn't believe it as the minutes ticked past. *What is wrong with them?* There was no one there to see them outside Mr Carson's office. For once, they didn't have to worry about what anyone else would think. *Just say something!* Olivia wanted to scream at them both.

She gritted her teeth. *I can't stand this. I have to see what's going on!*

Moving as stealthily as she could, she inched around the corner. When she was sure they weren't looking, she scooted at top speed to the other side of the doorway and hid behind a large potted plant. *Whew. I made it!*

They couldn't see her, but she could see them . . . *And talk about a depressing sight!*

Finn and Amelia sat with a single chair between them, so close they could have reached out and touched. But they were both pretending to be completely alone! Amelia stared pointedly at the ceiling. Finn sat staring at the ground, absentmindedly rolling the wheels of his skateboard again and again . . .

'Would you mind not doing that?' Amelia asked eventually. 'The noise is going straight through me.' She rubbed her temples as though she had a headache.

'Sorry.' Finn sighed. 'I was just checking them. I screwed the wheels back in earlier, but I need to make sure they're in good shape. I don't want to have an accident.'

Amelia gave a small smile. 'I thought you skater-boys liked to live dangerously.'

Look up! Olivia wanted to scream at Finn. *She's smiling at you, can't you see?*

Finn shrugged, still looking at the ground. 'We do. But there's a difference between "dangerous" and "stupid".'

'And the difference is . . . ?'

'Um . . .' Finn's lips curved into a rueful smile. For the first time, he darted a glance at Amelia. 'I don't know. Hope that doesn't mean *I'm* stupid!'

Amelia's face quivered. Her lips – *Yes!* Olivia cheered silently. Amelia's lips were definitely twitching! She was trying not to let her smile become a huge grin.

Do it! Olivia silently urged the other girl. *Give in!*

'I'm sure you're not stupid,' Amelia said softly. Olivia had never heard her sounding so sweet! Her cheeks were blushing now. Finn was staring at her, his mouth hanging half-open. Olivia could see what he was thinking – it was written all over his face. *Amelia is being nice to me!*

Fabulous! Olivia thought. *My plan is actually working. Now, all I need is for Amelia to look at him again and give him one of her beautiful smiles.*

But instead, Amelia's face straightened. She looked back up at the ceiling, and the moment passed. Two chairs away, Finn shrugged and went back to rolling the wheels of the board. *Creak! Creak!*

Amelia's right, Olivia thought glumly. *That really is quite irritating.*

But what was even more irritating was the fact that the two of them were wasting their perfect opportunity. Were they really going to let this moment slip through their fingertips without saying another word to each other?

Had she made a terrible mistake setting this up? She'd been so sure they liked each other. But . . .

Wait! What's that?

Finn wasn't looking at the ground any more. His gaze had turned . . . to Amelia. And he wasn't looking away.

Olivia held her breath as she turned to look for the Goth-Queen's reaction.

Amelia had definitely noticed, too. Her eyes might still be fixed on the ceiling, but her normally-pale skin was flushing pink. And as

Olivia watched, Amelia ever-so-casually lifted her left hand out of her lap and laid it on the empty chair between them.

Yes, yes, yes! Olivia willed Finn. *Take her hand. Just do it!*

Finn's own cheeks had flushed now, too. His gaze rested on Amelia's hand. Slowly, slo-o-o-owly, his own right hand lifted to hover in the air just above hers. His gaze flicked to Amelia's. She didn't look at him, but she didn't move her hand, either. Gradually, his hand began to lower over hers . . .

Loud footsteps sounded in the hallway behind Olivia. She spun around. *Oh, no.* It was Principal Carson!

She lunged down the hallway to intercept him. *He can't go into the office. Not now!*

She thudded to a halt in front of him just before he could turn the corner. 'Mr Carson!' she gasped.

'Olivia Abbott?' Frowning down at her, the principal came to a halt. 'What is it?'

Olivia gulped. *I forgot how tall he is!*

As he loomed over her, broad and intimidating in his sharply creased grey suit, he blocked out the light. 'Um . . .' Olivia's head whirled, then went completely blank. 'Uh . . .' *Why didn't I come up with a plan for this part?*

He shook his head impatiently. 'Miss Abbott, if there's something you'd like to say to me, please do so.' He looked over her head. 'Otherwise –'

'There is! There is something I wanted to say.'

'I see.' He sighed and began to move around her. 'Shall we discuss it in my office?'

'No!' She almost leaped to plant herself in front of him again, blocking his way. 'This can't wait. I have to . . . um . . .' Her thoughts whirled. 'I have to complain about my homework!'

'I beg your pardon?' He blinked.

Inwardly, Olivia winced at what she was about to do. But she had no choice – Finn and Amelia's meet-cute moment had to be protected at all costs. If Olivia could get the two of them together, she could unite the whole school, which meant that she and Ivy might actually be able to hang out again. Like twins should. It was crazy that they were split apart!

Pretend you're Jessica Phelps, she thought. *Just say exactly what she would say. She wouldn't worry about embarrassing herself!*

She drew herself up. 'Do you realise how much homework my teachers want me to do while I'm *on-set* next week?' she demanded. 'Don't any of you understand I have commitments and responsibilities? I am a movie star, you know?'

. . . *And I sound like a stuck-up witch!* she finished miserably, to herself.

Mr Carson gave her a weary smile. 'I understand

you are under a lot of pressure, Miss Abbott, especially for someone so young. What you must remember, though, is that your education is still primary, even above your film commitments. You really wouldn't want to fall behind.' He started to move around her. 'And now –'

'No!' Cringing inwardly, Olivia turned her nose up in the air. 'I have to warn you, Principal Carson, you *will* be hearing from my agent about this!'

If I still have an agent, anyway. She hadn't spoken to Amy Teller for so long, even Olivia wasn't sure about it!

'I'm sure I will,' Mr Carson said. 'But for now, just worry about getting to your homework done *on time*, please, Miss Abbott.'

He walked past her briskly, and Olivia sagged. Reluctantly, she began to walk away, moving as slowly as possible. She came to a stop, though, when she heard Mr Carson step into his office. 'Mr Jorgensen. And . . .?' He sounded surprised. 'Why are you here, Miss Thompson?'

Amelia sounded as haughty as ever as she replied, 'I was told that you wanted to see me.'

'Well, unless you can tell me exactly which teacher sent you here, you should get off home,' Mr Carson said. 'At least, unlike Mr Jorgensen, you don't take inappropriate *toys* to school.'

'Sir, my board isn't a toy!' Finn protested.

'Save it for the office,' Mr Carson drawled. 'And now, Miss Thompson, if you don't mind . . .?'

Amelia's annoyed sigh was so loud, it carried down the hall. *Uh-oh*, Olivia thought. *Time to get out of sight. Fast!*

She scampered as quickly as she could through the hallway, ducking and diving around corners until she made it out through a side door of the school. As she pushed the door open, she darted a glance backwards, just to make sure Amelia wasn't heading in her direction. Luckily, Amelia was nowhere in sight . . . but as Olivia tumbled through the door, she ran straight into a stinky leather trench coat that almost smothered her.

'I'm so sorry!' She stumbled back, crinkling her nose at the stench. *Has this boy ever showered?*

The tall, wiry older boy she'd collided with was as goth as they came – his coat had to weigh more than he did – but he had the same unwashed stench she remembered from Garrick Stephens and the other middle school 'Beasts'. *No, it's even worse*, Olivia realised. *It's a more mature version – so it's even fouler!*

Instead of scowling like one of the Beasts, though, he gave her a smirk that made her take another step backwards.

'Don't you worry, sweetie-pie,' he drawled, in an obviously fake growly voice. 'You're not the first girl to have a crush on me.' His grin deepened. He twitched up the collar of his trench coat under his long, lank, oily-looking hair. '. . . And you probably won't be the last, either. I am a *chick magnet.*'

Eww! Olivia couldn't help the shudder that wracked her. 'Sorry!' she mumbled. Ducking her head, she hurried past him, ignoring his laughter . . . But it was harder to ignore his smell, which followed her all the way down the path. It seemed to have soaked right into her clothing with the collision.

Now I need another shower, too!

Olivia's plan had come so close to working . . . only to be ruined at the crucial moment.

Chapter Six

It's hard to believe, Ivy admitted to herself, *but I'm actually starting to like this skatepark.*

She was back at the park in Lincoln Vale yet again, doing her job as Sophia's best friend. Thank darkness, Sophia had finally realised just how silly she'd been over Finn. Ivy couldn't have been happier or more relieved that Sophia had emerged from that debacle with her heart in one piece . . . But she was definitely changed by it. Ivy shook her head as she looked at the lightning-haired figure zooming down the middle of the skatepark.

Who could ever have imagined that Sophia would turn out to genuinely love skateboarding? Talk about an un-vampire-like activity!

As Ivy watched, Sophia flipped her board up at the end of a spectacular trick that made the older skater-boys all break into spontaneous applause.

At least she's gotten better at it. Smiling, Ivy shook her head. Two weeks into high school, and elegant goth vampire Sophia was turning into a skateboard master – while Ivy had realised that the skatepark was the only safe place to study! Few of the Lincoln Vale goths loitered here, and the skater-boys had no interest in anything beyond their boards . . . well, and in Sophia, who was currently giving them all tips on how to perform her trick!

For once, Ivy didn't have a single groupie racing to impress her . . . and she couldn't have been happier about that. Right now, she really needed to finish her English assignment! Mr Russell wanted them all to read poems out in Friday's class, and Ivy still hadn't managed to choose one yet.

Sighing, she forced herself to look away from Sophia's triumph and go back to flipping through the pages of her textbook. Ivy liked English – well, she liked middle school English, because she'd understood that more – but honestly . . . was every poem in this book written by someone in a seriously bad mood? Not every poet in all of history had been a vampire, had they?

'Can I sit next to you?' The goth-girl who'd suddenly appeared at Ivy's side looked every bit as glum as a vampire poet. Her voice reeked of hopelessness.

Ivy narrowed her eyes. Was this girl a vampire? Her brown eyes looked genuine, not like contact lenses, so probably not. Unfortunately, that still left 'groupie' as a serious possibility.

Ivy looked at thc rest of the large picnic table and gave up. She didn't have any good excuses to offer. 'Sure,' she said. 'But I'm busy with homework right now.'

'That's OK.' The girl – her name was Penny Taylor, Ivy remembered now, from English class – sat down across from Ivy, dumping her black backpack on the table. It was studded with steel nubs and bleeding heart symbols, and Penny drooped even more as she looked down at it. 'I like to sit in silence with people,' she said, sounding miserable. 'It gives me time to reflect. And to ponder things. Dark things.'

Did she seriously just use the word 'ponder' in a sentence? Ivy stopped herself just in time from asking exactly what 'dark things' Penny liked to ponder. That had the potential to be death-squint irritating!

Unless . . . She frowned. Was this girl for real, or did she actually have a dry sense of humour? If this super-goth pose was a joke, Ivy could kind of appreciate it. But . . .

'Look . . .' Penny sighed heavily. 'A whole park full of people looking in the other direction.' She turned to gaze soulfully at Ivy. 'Do you ever feel that everyone in the *world* is looking in the other direction?'

Right now, it feels like everyone is looking right at me, Ivy thought. She had to bite down hard on her tongue to keep the words from coming out. Then she twitched with pain. *Ouch!* Her too-sharp fangs had just drawn blood. She stifled a moan as she put one hand to her cheek.

With a glance at Ivy's poetry textbook, Penny reached into her backpack and pulled out her own. The front was covered with doodles – headstones and daggers, barbed wire and skulls –

and from the shy look Penny gave her, Ivy knew she was supposed to comment on them.

'Wow, that's . . . very goth.' Ivy gave a polite smile. 'I can certainly tell which gang you belong to at school.'

'Really?' Light broke through the mask of misery on Penny's face. Beaming, she pulled up her shirt sleeve. 'Here, look! I just got this today.'

Obediently, Ivy leaned over and saw the temporary tattoo on Penny's wrist: a ram's skull with twisted horns. *Seriously? She's showing off a temporary tattoo?* 'Um . . . yeah,' she finally managed. 'Nice.'

It was true that Ivy liked all things Gothic . . . But weren't temporary tattoos a bit childish?

Even if she'd been rude enough to say so, though, she couldn't have gotten a word in edgeways. It was as if her admiration of Penny's doodles had opened up a dam, and now all of

Penny's words were flooding out.

'You wouldn't believe where I went yesterday,' Penny said. 'A record store – can you believe it? Real, old-school vinyl in a real-life record store! I even managed to track down the EP of Death Rattle's first live gig. That is seriously rare! Rare like a . . . a really rare steak!' She lifted one hand to her mouth.

Is she about to be sick? Ivy stared at the other girl. 'Ohh-kay.'

'But we were talking about music!' Penny visibly perked up. 'You've heard of Death Rattle, right? They are an incredibly important goth band! Oh, and there are lots of other important goth bands, too. There's the Pall Bearers, and . . .'

Ivy shook her head wonderingly as Penny listed off on her fingers every goth band she knew. *It's like she's been cramming for a goth exam!*

'Wow,' she said, finally breaking through the list.

'You must be the ultimate student.'

'Oh, no.' Penny's face crumpled. 'Was it too much? A step too far?'

Ivy blinked. 'Too much of what?' she asked. 'I don't understand.'

'Oh, forget it! You don't have to pretend.' Penny's eyes brimmed with tears. 'I knew you'd see through my act!' she said. 'Someone as cool as you . . . of course you'd know a genuine goth from a fake goth. I should never have even bothered trying. I'm such a loser!' With a sob, she buried her face in her hands.

'Hey!' Shaking her head, Ivy hurried to the other side of the table to put a hand on Penny's shoulder. 'I don't even know what's going on!' she protested. 'Are you telling me this was all an act? You're not even a real goth?'

Penny nodded without uncovering her face.

'But what's the point?' Ivy slumped on to the

seat beside Penny, her head whirling. 'Who would pretend to be a goth?'

'I hate goth stuff,' Penny mumbled. 'I hate the colour black. It's so ugly! I like pink, sparkly things.'

'Really?' Ivy looked at Penny's dyed-black hair and all-black outfit and let out a snort of laughter. 'You should meet my sister, then.'

I just wish she was here now. Ivy sighed. How long had it been since she and Olivia had managed to have a heart-to-heart like this one? *It's ridiculous that ever since school started, I've had less time with my own twin than I do with any random goth!*

That wasn't Penny's fault, though. Gathering her wayward thoughts, Ivy said briskly, 'No wonder you've been acting so miserable. You must feel absolutely suffocated!'

'I do,' Penny said. 'But it doesn't matter.' She lifted her tear-streaked face out of her hands, sniffing. 'I can't stand to be disliked at school. Haven't you seen how the pink girls are treated?' She drew a deep breath, sniffing back the last of her tears. 'I won't let it happen to me. I have to be liked . . . and if that means faking goth, that's just what I have to do!'

Ivy stared at her in disbelief for a long moment. Then she let her head fall on to the table with a clunk. 'This high school is even crazier than I'd thought!'

'I just want to be popular,' Penny whispered. 'Is that so bad?'

Ivy groaned. 'Trust me. I would happily hand my popularity over to you any day.'

Penny shook her head sadly. 'That's the problem. You can't buy and sell popularity, can you? It's not a commodity. You have to have . . .' she waved a hand through the air and snapped her black-tipped fingers '. . . *je ne sais quoi.*'

'*Je ne sais* . . . what?' Ivy repeated, blinking.

Penny sighed. 'You have it . . . and I just don't.' Scooping up the notebook and her backpack, she shook her head. 'I should never have even bothered trying.'

Her shoulders drooped as she walked away . . . and Ivy felt her stomach sink as she watched.

This is ridiculous. She couldn't just watch Penny suffer under the school's idiotic social rules. There had to be some way for Ivy to share some of her popularity with Penny . . .

And better yet, she realised, *if it works, it might just deflect some of the attention away from me!*

Chapter Seven

The next morning, Ivy walked into school with a plan . . . and a *swagger.*

This had better work, she told herself.

She'd been up late last night perfecting her 'don't-come-near-me' walk, up and down the landing. She hadn't planned to do it on her own, but Olivia's cell phone had been turned off when Ivy had tried to call her for help – and being out of touch with her twin *again* had only made Ivy more determined. *I have to fix this!*

She would have kept going even longer, but just after midnight, her dad had emerged from his room, elegant as always in his black satin pyjamas, and politely asked her to please, *for darkness' sake*, go to her coffin and get some sleep!

It had been worth the late night, though. With a really arrogant swagger, Ivy would definitely put off groupies. *This is exactly what I need to stall out my popularity at this school!*

Unfortunately, her swagger required her to keep her chin and nose up in the air, which made it more than a little difficult to walk, especially in the crowded school hallway. She couldn't see a single thing on the ground . . .

Like the leg of an older boy in an absolutely *ludicrous* leather trench coat, sticking out for no other reason than to trip up a stranger!

Ivy's legs flew out beneath her. Flailing for balance, she would have fallen flat on her face if she'd been a human . . . but, taken off guard, her vampire reflexes took over. Before she could stop herself, she sprang into a front-flip and landed neatly on her feet.

All around her, students broke into spontaneous applause.

'Oh, Ivy!'

'That was amazing!'

'How did you do that?'

'You are *soooooo cool*!'

Aaaargh! Ivy bit back a scream of frustration. *Why didn't I let myself fall on my face?*

It was as if the whole universe was conspiring to make her more and more popular, whether she liked it or not!

Growling, she stalked over to the older boy, who was snickering with his friends.

'Oops,' he said. 'Did I trip you? I must not have seen you coming. Heh.'

Even Garrick Stephens, the head of the middle school Beasts, would have found this boy's grin repulsive. His stench battered her sensitive vampire senses, but Ivy walked straight up to glare at him.

'You'd have a lot more luck seeing where not to stick your legs,' she told him, 'if your hair wasn't greasy enough to cook French fries on!'

'Ooooohhhh.' The students behind her let out a collective gasp.

'Did you hear what she said to Josh?'

'She is so brave!'

The older boy – Josh – glared back at her. Stepping closer, he opened his mouth as if to say something.

Ivy narrowed her eyes into a death-squint . . . and Josh paled. Stepping back, he cowered against the lockers.

'That's better,' she told him, and turned away.

As she walked into homeroom, she could hear him complaining to his friends. 'If I'd known this school was a haven for crazies, I would never have transferred here!'

Whatever. Ivy rolled her eyes. She couldn't escape the groupies all clustering around her now, though, as she headed for her desk at the back of the room. The goths pushed and shoved past each other to clap her on the back in congratulations, while the bunnies hung back, gazing at her with big, dazzled-looking eyes.

'You were so awesome!'

'The whole school is going to be glad you took Josh down a peg. He's deserved it ever since he started here.'

'He probably deserved it at his last school, too.'

'You're such a hero!'

Across the room, Ivy glimpsed her twin finally walking in. *Thank darkness for a voice of common sense!* She waved eagerly – but with the mass of followers surrounding her, they might as well have been miles apart. Olivia's gaze passed over the crowd, and she sighed. Giving a sad half-smile, she went to join Sophia without even making a move in Ivy's direction.

She's probably right. They'd never have let her through to me.

Grimacing, Ivy sat down at her desk, desperate for the teacher to walk in and force everyone else to disperse. How many more pats on the back could she take before it bruised? *So much for my plan to stall out my popularity.*

As she looked around for the teacher, she caught Penny Taylor's eye.

The pseudo-goth-girl sat alone near the front of the class, looking horribly alone. The desks on both sides of her were empty, and as she watched the other students crowd around Ivy, her eyes glimmered with wistfulness.

I have to do something, Ivy realised. *But what?*

She still hadn't figured out what to do by the end of the morning. But as she walked towards the cafeteria for lunch, she glanced out a window and saw Penny sitting alone in a quiet corner outside, reading a familiar-looking magazine. Ivy couldn't see what the magazine was called, but she knew exactly who it was aimed at: girly, teeny-bop bunnies. It pretty much had to be, because it had a picture of her sister's boyfriend on the front cover!

Pushing open the closest door, Ivy stepped outside. Penny gasped and slammed the magazine shut. 'I wasn't really reading it! I was just . . .'

'Does the article on Jackson mention Olivia?' Ivy asked. She pointed to the picture of Jackson's smiling face. 'If it does, I might have to buy it.'

'Oh, well . . . um . . . I mean, I wasn't really reading it. I mean, not for pleasure. I just . . .'

Ivy raised one eyebrow as Penny stammered to a halt. 'I saw you smiling as you turned the pages.'

'Um, that was an *ironic* smile.' Penny swallowed visibly. 'A pitying smile! At how silly the articles in these magazines are. You know. Mainstream? They should – they should call it *lamestream*!'

Ivy rolled her eyes. 'You shared your secret with me, remember? I know you like the lighter side of life. It's OK, I won't tell anyone.'

'Well . . .' Penny relaxed. She gave a guilty-looking grin. 'The truth is,' she admitted, 'the "Have You Spotted?" section is quite entertaining, if . . . oh!' She gave a sudden gasp and clamped her mouth shut.

Ivy looked around. *Aha.* A group of goth-girls was sidling towards them, obviously trying to eavesdrop on their conversation. *Penny's scared of blowing her cover. Which means . . .*

Moving with vampire speed, Ivy snatched the magazine from Penny's hands. 'See?' she said, pointing. 'That's the part I wanted you to look at.'

Penny stared at her. Then her face lit up with gratitude. 'Oh,' she said. '*Oh!* You mean, in *your* magazine.'

'That's right.' Ivy smiled as the other goths reached them. Pointedly, she turned the bubblegum-coloured cover directly towards them. 'I was just showing Penny something I really liked in *my* magazine.'

Come on, she silently urged the other goths. *Start sneering! See, I'm not cool after all, am I?*

One goth raised her eyebrows. But she didn't sneer. Instead, she looked thoughtful. The others peered closer.

'Is that magazine cool?'

'*I've* been reading that magazine forever!'

'Maybe I'll get a copy after school.'

Argh! Ivy screamed silently.

Next to her, though, Penny was leaning into the circle of other girls with wistful delight, like a plant stretching towards the sunlight. *That's it*, Ivy decided. *I have to shift this school's attention on to Penny. Let* her *be the cool one!*

And the time to make that change was . . . *now*. Because the hovering goth-girls were already beginning to swarm! *Where are they all coming from?* Ivy wondered, as more and more flooded through the school doors towards her.

'Ivy, why aren't you going to lunch? Aren't you hungry?'

'Maybe she doesn't want to.'

'Is lunch "uncool" now?' one goth-girl gasped.

Ivy stared at her in disbelief. *How could not having lunch be cool?* She shook her head. 'I'm not skipping lunch. I was just stopping here to . . .

to . . .' Inspiration struck. 'To ask Penny for some fashion advice!'

'Really?' The goth-girls flocked closer, looking from Ivy to Penny and back.

'Oh, yes.' Ivy nodded solemnly. 'Penny is the one girl at this school with real *style*. Don't you think?'

'Oohhh . . .' There was a collective sigh as all the girls clustered around Penny, looking her up and down, from her black lace T-shirt and silver dragon bracelet to her skinny black jeans and boots.

Penny's cheeks were flushed, but she looked desperately hopeful. Ivy gave her a firm nod of support. 'I always think that Penny looks just right.'

'I do like your style,' the closest goth-girl said to Penny.

'Oh . . . me, too.'

'And me.'

It's working! Ivy thought . . .

. . . Until the goth-girls turned away from Penny to beam at Ivy.

'You're so *perceptive*, Ivy!'

'You notice *everything*!'

'Of *course* Ivy was the one who noticed that Penny wasn't just a normal goth!'

At least that part's true, Ivy thought glumly. *But only in ways that these girls don't realise!*

The girls were all flocking back to her now. 'How can *we* learn to see people the way you do, Ivy?' another goth-girl sighed wistfully.

I can't take this any more! Losing her cool completely, Ivy gave in to sarcasm. Waving her hands, she droned, '*O . . . pen . . . your . . . eyes . . .*'

But even blatant rudeness didn't work.

'You're *so* right, Ivy.'

'Of course she's right!'

'I *will* open my eyes and see people better. I swear it!'

'If only there were glasses or contact lenses that helped us see *true* style,' one of the girls mused. 'If some scientist could invent that, they'd be a gazillionaire . . . and they'd deserve it!'

Another girl snorted. 'But would they be able to come up with a de-pinking ray? Something to rid the world of all perkiness?'

Penny flushed, suddenly looking down at her hands, but the other girls were too busy laughing and cheering the idea on to notice.

'Who *wouldn't* buy a de-pinking ray?'

'*My sister* wouldn't,' Ivy snapped.

An awkward silence fell over the group. As the other girls slid her frightened glances, Ivy realised she had gone too far. Her tone hadn't just been dismissive – it had been downright scary.

She forced a laugh. 'So, anyway –'

'Ohh!' One of the girls gasped, pointing. 'Are you wearing joke vampire teeth?'

Oh, no. Busted! Ivy slammed her mouth shut . . . but it was too late. Everybody had already seen her fangs.

'That is so cool!'

'But Ivy, the teachers will have a fit if they notice them!'

'That's why Ivy's so cool. She doesn't care about authority!'

No, she's just really, really behind on her dental work, Ivy thought grimly.

She couldn't delay any longer. She had to get to the vampire dentist *tonight.*

Olivia giggled into her cell phone as she walked up Undertaker Hill that evening. The air was cool and scented with flowers, there was a comfortable hum of activity in the houses nearby . . . and she was talking to her favourite boy in the world, who'd just called unexpectedly.

'You've finally managed a perfect Cockney accent!' she said, on hearing his voice.

'I know,' Jackson said mournfully. 'Too bad I'll never need it again, now that we're all finished filming the scenes with the British twins!'

Spotting Ivy's house ahead, Olivia slowed her steps to prolong the phone call. 'Where are you calling from, anyway?'

'Um . . . somewhere?' Jackson yawned. 'Sorry. I'm on the road in one of Mr Harker's cars, and I only just woke up. I can't see any signs on the highway right now . . . so I'm not really sure where I am!'

'Well, I'm glad you called me, wherever you are,' Olivia murmured.

'I'll always call you.' Jackson's voice was firm. 'Wherever I am.'

'I know.' Olivia smiled as they said their goodbyes. Even after she'd hung up, she stood still for a moment, basking in contentment.

She was home, where she belonged; but she still had Jackson, and their relationship was so much better now *because* of the time they'd had away from each other. She could now end a call without feeling fraught, because she *knew* that he loved her no matter what . . . and she knew, too, that she was happier for being here in Franklin Grove, rather than being caught up in the hectic movie star lifestyle.

Maybe someday, when she was older, she would change her mind . . . but for now, she was so much happier to have a normal life. *Whatever 'normal' is in Franklin Grove, anyway!*

Taking a deep breath, she slipped her cell phone back into her bag and hurried up the steps to Ivy's house. Maybe things had felt weird with her twin for the past few days, but it was time to break down the barriers of silence that had built up between them. After all, when the worst came to the worst, she knew Ivy would *always* have her back . . . wouldn't she?

She didn't help me when those goths were sneering at me at her lunch table, a little voice whispered in the back of Olivia's head.

Gritting her teeth, she forced the thought aside. *I'm sure there's a reasonable explanation for that*, she told herself. *I'll find out when we finally get to talk about it.* And they didn't just need to clear up their own issues. Right now, Olivia needed the most popular girl in her grade to help with her 'Famelia' problem!

When the door opened, though, it wasn't Ivy who stood there. It was Lillian.

'Olivia!' Lillian smiled warmly. 'How are you?'

'Oh . . . um . . . fine,' Olivia mumbled.

She'd been working so hard to prepare herself for a heart-to-heart with Ivy, it was a shock to see anyone different. She craned her neck to look past their stepmom. 'Is Ivy here?'

'No, she's gone to the dentist for an emergency touch-up.'

'What?' Olivia's gaze flashed back up in surprise. 'At this time of day?'

Lillian gave a wink. 'Not a *regular* dentist. You know how it is.'

'Ohhhh. Of course.' Olivia forced a laugh, as embarrassment crashed down on her. 'I should have known.'

The truth was, she *didn't* know how it was. She'd never minded being the only non-vampire when she was with Ivy and their dad. But somehow, it felt worse to be out of the loop when she was around her elegant new vampire stepmom.

'Why don't you come in and wait for her?' Lillian stepped back to let her in.

'OK. Thanks.' Olivia drew a deep breath and followed Lillian into the kitchen, her thoughts whirling. If Ivy wasn't here, who could she talk to about her plans for 'Famelia'?

What about my bio-dad?

Of course! Charles Vega would definitely know how to resolve a star-crossed love affair – because he'd had the *ultimate* impossible romance with their mom!

'Is Dad here?' she asked.

'Oh, I'm afraid he's out running some errands.' Lillian reached into the refrigerator and took out the juice that was always kept stocked there for Olivia's visits.

'Oh.' Olivia slumped.

Lillian raised her eyebrows comically. 'Don't look so disappointed,' she said, faking outrage.

'Sorry,' said Olivia, laughing with her. 'I've just got some stuff on my mind.'

'Anything I can help with?' Lillian asked.

Olivia thought for a split-second of a split-second. How could she not have realised before? Lillian had worked in movies for decades. She was the *perfect* person to help navigate the story of 'Famelia'!

As the two of them snacked on tortilla chips and salsa, Olivia gave her stepmom all the details. Luckily, Lillian was already fluent in Camilla-ese, so it was easy to sum up what had already happened. 'I think they're just about halfway through their Act Two,' Olivia finished, 'but they're still not together. What can I do?'

'Well . . .' Tapping her chip on her plate, Lillian looked pensive. 'There are *always* obstacles in every rom-com, you know. If the "meet-cute" didn't work, maybe what they need now is to be shown the "awful alternatives". You know, that moment in movies and TV when the hero and heroine go on dates with really *horrible* people. It helps them realise who they really love.'

'Hmm.' Olivia crunched her chip thoughtfully. 'I think that actually might work . . . and that way, no one needs to get a lecture from the principal! Thank you!'

I have such a cool stepmom, she realised.

Chapter Eight

Ivy grimaced as she stepped back into the Slice of Life pizza parlour and saw a life-size plastic cockroach in the corner, near a mouldy-looking smear of old tomato sauce.

I know they have to make this place look gross, she thought. *But did they have to do such a good job of it?* Her mouth tasted funny enough from the procedure she'd just undergone downstairs, without adding so many other horrible flavours to the air!

To all the bunnies of Franklin Grove, the Slice of Life was known as the nastiest pizza parlour in the universe. None of them could understand how it had stayed in business for so long.

Only the vampires knew the truth: that the Slice of Life's disgusting appearance was exactly what made it the perfect base for Dr Pane Lee, the town's resident vampire dentist. Dr Lee kept his practice in the basement, and the vampires of Franklin Grove went in and out freely throughout the night, pretending to be visiting the twenty-four-hour pizza parlour.

I almost wish I had been, Ivy thought glumly. Sure, the Slice of Life looked awful. But could eating mouldy pizza really be that much worse than having her super-long fangs filed with Dr Lee's 'special machine', the one he only reserved for really drastic cases? She shuddered at the memory of the grinding noise it had made, rattling through her bones.

Worse yet, the polish he'd added at the end

tasted of *pink bubblegum.* Talk about a bunny flavour!

Hunching her shoulders, Ivy ran her tongue over her newly-short fangs and fought the urge to gag at the taste as it mingled with the disgusting smells of the pizza parlour. *It's definitely time to get back outside!*

Ignoring the cobwebs and fake roaches that cluttered the corners, Ivy walked past the dust-covered service counter where Rachel, the 'manageress' of the Slice of Life – who was actually Dr Lee's receptionist – was pretending to read a sauce-spattered magazine.

Cobwebs trailed off Rachel's dirty cap, which was topped by a plastic spider, and a smear of red – which Ivy's sensitive nose identified as paint rather than real pizza sauce – spread all the way across her cheek. As Ivy passed, Rachel looked up just long enough to give a secret nod . . .

before ticking off a note in the patient book that was hidden inside the magazine.

Nodding back, Ivy held her breath and picked her way across the spills of dried cheese that covered the floor. It was a huge relief to reach the doorway. On the threshold, she started to turn back to wave goodbye to Rachel . . .

And then the unthinkable happened. From the corner of her eye she saw a hand . . . a hand reaching for the door.

Reaching for the door to the Slice of Life? I must be seeing things!

Ivy squeezed her eyes shut. Then she opened them, blinking hard . . . and saw the door being pulled all the way open.

She spun around. *Oh, no!*

It was an older boy – a high school senior, judging by his appearance, but she'd never seen him before. *He must go to Willowton*, she realised.

But what is he thinking, for darkness' sake? Are they even crazier at Willowton than at Franklin Grove? No one in their right mind would ever try to eat here! It has been designed specially, to repel all non-vamps!

But the boy wasn't alone. He had run ahead to hold the door open for a whole group of his friends, who were all talking and laughing as they hurried down the street towards him . . . and even though he raised his eyebrows as he peered inside, he didn't turn away. Instead, he called to his friends.

'Come on. It doesn't look all that bad. We might as well give it a try.'

Ivy squared her shoulders. *I can't let this happen!*

Every vampire in Franklin Grove knew that they had a duty to keep bunnies out of the Slice of Life, to keep them from seeing or hearing something they shouldn't . . . Last summer, Ivy and Brendan had started an impromptu 'Ketchup

War' in the street to scare off a bunny couple who looked like they might give it a try. It had actually been fun – until Rachel asked them to help clean up!

Ivy spun around and yelled at Rachel: 'That food was *disgusting*! How dare you try to charge me for something that had bugs in it?'

The boy holding the door stepped back. Ivy heard his friends' footsteps slowing. Someone halfway down the street whispered, 'Did she just say *bugs*?'

Rachel yelled back, 'Oh, come on, at least most of the bugs on your pizza were dead.'

'Some of them were still moving!' Ivy declared. 'In my mouth!'

The boy let go of the door, swallowing visibly. Ivy lifted her chin. 'This is a scandal. I'm not paying you. I'm reporting you to the health board! Just as soon as I . . . as I . . .'

She clapped her hand to her mouth. Bending over, she forced her shoulders to heave.

Running footsteps sounded down the street outside as the boy and his friends fled at top speed.

Behind the counter, Rachel chuckled. 'Well done,' she said. 'Are you sure it's your sister who's the actress in the family?'

Ivy snorted as she straightened up. 'Positive.'

Shaking her head, she walked outside and took a deep breath of the clean air. Her mouth was still tingling, but at least she could breathe now. She just wished she could erase her memories of the last half hour as easily as she'd gotten rid of those would-be pizza customers.

Sure, she'd had some bad dental procedures in the past . . . but Dr Lee had never before had to kneel on the armrest just to file down her fangs, much less take out his 'special machine'! And the lecture he'd given her afterwards had made her feel even worse. She frowned, kicking at the pavement as she remembered how angry he'd been at her for waiting too long between filings.

'This isn't just a matter of personal comfort, young lady. It's about protecting the secrets of the whole vampire race!'

'Stupid high school,' she muttered now. If it hadn't been for how crazy her stupid popularity was making her, she would never have let it go for this long . . .

Nice try, Ivy. She sighed, giving up. Even to herself, she couldn't pretend that it was anyone's fault but her own. Keeping her fangs filed was basic vampire concealment strategy, and it had to take priority over everything else. No matter what was going on at school, she should never have neglected it.

The whole thing felt so depressing that for once, Ivy couldn't even bring herself to feel hungry for dinner. She'd already arranged to meet Brendan at the Meat and Greet, though, so she trudged through the dark street towards the brightly lit diner, trying to ignore the sickly sweet taste left in her mouth by the tooth filing.

Brendan was waiting for her at one of the booths in the back, along with two steaming-hot, rare burgers. 'Well, look at that.' He grinned as he pulled open her mouth to peer dramatically at her teeth. 'No more horror movie material!'

'Get off!' Laughing, Ivy pushed his hand away and settled in next to him, ignoring her waiting burger. 'I don't want to even think about teeth for at least a month.'

'Really, it's too bad.' As Brendan picked up his own burger, he gave a mock sigh. 'I'm going to miss those fangs. You're so beautiful when you're scary.'

'Why does everyone at school seem to think that?' Ivy groaned and dropped her head on to the table beside her plate. 'I've been doing my scariest "Leave Me Alone" act all week, and it's just not working! I don't know what else to try.'

'Well . . .' Brendan's tone turned wary. 'I think I might know what's wrong.'

'Yeah?' Ivy turned her head to glance up at him.

Brendan took a deep breath. 'I think your heart's not really in it.'

'*What?*' Ivy jerked upright. 'What are you talking about? You *know* I hate this popularity trap!'

'But think about what you're doing to escape it. Snubbing people? Making fun of others?' Brendan's tone was gentle as he reached out to put one hand on top of hers. 'Come on, Ivy. Yes, you're a loner – and yeah, you take things pretty seriously – but you've never been *mean* before.'

Ivy swallowed hard, staring down at her burger as guilt clenched her chest. 'I'm not sure about that,' she mumbled. 'I've been known to be pretty grumpy.'

'Maybe so,' Brendan said, 'but you're not acting like yourself. That's why you've been so unhappy.' He squeezed her hand. 'The truth is, you're the *anti*-mean. Deliberately hurting other people's feelings . . . that's just not in your nature.'

He waited a moment, but Ivy couldn't answer. She was fighting too hard against the sudden knot in her chest . . . the one that said he was right.

'That whole scene at lunch where you made fun of that poor girl's T-shirt?' Brendan's voice was soft, but inescapable. 'I've never seen you mock anyone to their face before. That's not you. Is it?'

'No,' Ivy whispered. Her throat clenched. She turned her hand over to lace her fingers through his. 'It's not,' she agreed. 'But I don't know what else to do. All I want is to be left in peace! I want to be allowed to hang out with my own twin without half the school trying to get in between us.'

'Trust me,' Brendan said. 'Everything will work out if you just *stop pretending.*'

Pretending . . . Ivy froze as she connected the dots. Hadn't she told Penny the same thing? Penny was working so hard to pretend to be another person, it was making her miserable. And Ivy had been doing just the same, without even realising it. In fact . . .

She winced. This morning in the courtyard, when they'd been with all the other goths, she had actually been . . . kind-of-sort-of-a-little-bit . . . *making* Penny pretend even more than she already had been.

Ouch. She sighed. *I can't do this any more – not to Penny or myself.*

One way or another, she was going to find a way to improve things for both of them.

Fuelled by new determination, Ivy reached for her burger. 'Mmm!' As she savoured the bite, she carefully wiped the grease from her lips. *It's so much better to eat without fangs!* No more accidentally biting herself in the cheek when she ate, no more . . .

'Wait a minute.' Ivy narrowed her eyes as she saw Brendan looking mock-sad beside her. 'What is it? What's wrong now?'

'Ohhh . . .' Brendan sighed mournfully. 'I just miss your scary ketchup face! Do you think you could do it again, once more? Just for me?'

'*You!*' She snatched back up her greasy napkin. 'I'm going to spread grease all over your face for that.'

Even as they arm-wrestled, though, exploding with laughter, Ivy felt the tension drain straight out of her. She might not know yet just how to fix her unwanted popularity or to make it up to Olivia for the 'canteen-incident' . . . but somehow, shc was beginning to feel certain that everything would be OK.

Chapter Nine

Operation Famelia: go!

Olivia hunkered down in her seat on the Lincoln Vale bus the next morning, scoping out her materials. It had taken hard planning and a ridiculously early alarm call for her to make it all the way out to Lincoln Vale in time to catch this school bus, instead of riding her usual Franklin Grove bus along with Ivy, Brendan, and Sophia. But it had been worth it. It was time to take Lillian's advice and set up an Awful Alternative for Amelia, to make Finn look even better by comparison . . . and Olivia knew exactly who to choose.

Josh Dillon sat at the very back of the bus with his Beastly friends, but the stench from his trench coat emanated all thc way to Olivia's seat in the middle of the bus. *He is definitely the one*, she decided, as she breathed through her mouth to avoid the worst of the smell. They might have only met once, but sometimes, once was more than enough. She was absolutely certain that Josh had to be the most horrid boy in Amelia's grade.

If only she could force Amelia to spend some time with Josh, the Goth-Queen would have to realise how fantastic Finn was! And really, this mission was bigger than either one of them. Not only did Amelia and Finn both secretly want to get together – whether or not they would admit it – but their romance would help to unite the whole school . . . and allow one particular pink-loving bunny girl to publicly sit with her goth twin at lunchtime.

Olivia took a deep breath. *I have to get this right!*

Unfortunately, Amelia wasn't helping the plan. She sat at the very front of the bus, with her back to everyone . . . including Josh. *Turn around*, Olivia willed silently, as Josh and the others let out obnoxious brays of laughter in the back of the bus. *Turn around, look at Josh, turn around . . .*

It was no use. If Olivia left it up to the 'heroine' of this rom-com, Amelia would never even glimpse her Awful Alternative. *It's time to play the director*, Olivia told herself. *Make it happen!*

But how?

Aha. As Olivia watched, she saw the flick of a page in the corner of her eye – her seat mate reading a novel. *I know exactly what to do!*

Amelia loved the book of *Eternal Sunset*. How better to start a conversation with her than to talk about the movie? *Then, once I've got her talking, I can ask her what she thinks of Josh, and get her to take a good look at him . . . yes!*

Olivia jumped out of her seat, ignoring the rattling of the moving bus. As she headed up the aisle towards Amelia, she started practising her opening lines. *So, you're an* Eternal Sunset *fan . . .*

'What do you think you're doing?' the bus driver screeched.

The whole bus went silent. Olivia froze.

The driver was a middle-aged woman named Mrs Martin, and when Olivia had first stepped on to the bus, she'd barely said a word. Now, though, her face looked furious in the rear-view mirror.

'I see you standing up, young lady! What do you think you're doing, walking around on a moving bus? Do you want me to lose my licence?'

Gusts of nervous laughter swept around the bus as Olivia stuttered. 'Um . . . I, um . . . I just . . .'

'I don't care!' Still steering with her right hand, Mrs Martin jabbed her finger towards the one empty seat nearby – the seat next to Amelia. 'You sit down this instant, young lady. I will not tolerate this behaviour!'

Cringing, Olivia hurried to take the empty seat beside Amelia, feeling the eyes of all the other students on her.

'Sorry,' Olivia said weakly to Mrs Martin.

Amelia rolled her eyes and sighed heavily, even as she moved her bag to make space for Olivia to sit. 'What are you doing on this bus anyway?' the older girl asked. 'This is the Lincoln Vale bus. Don't you live in Franklin Grove?'

'Er . . .' Olivia hesitated halfway into the seat. The truth was, she'd set her alarm clock for five-thirty a.m. and walked all the way to the next town specifically to catch this bus. She could hardly tell Amelia that, though – she'd look like a super-meddler. 'I, um, stayed over at a friend's house. Last night. In Lincoln Vale,' she mumbled.

'And they're not here with you now?' Sighing, Amelia looked over Olivia's head at the bus driver. 'Come on, you'd better sit down before she has any more of a fit.' Shaking her head, Amelia turned to gaze out the bus window, obviously dismissing Olivia.

Wait! This isn't how it was supposed to go. Desperately, Olivia grabbed for her earlier plan. 'So!' she said brightly. 'Did you know there's more filming for *Eternal Sunset* starting next week? I'm flying out on Saturday afternoon.'

'Good for you,' Amelia drawled, still looking out the window.

Olivia forged on, trying to sound enthusiastic. 'We'll be shooting the futuristic dream sequences – oh, but I probably shouldn't talk too much about this, should I? I mean, unless you want to know the details . . .' She trailed her words off enticingly.

At just that moment, a familiar flash of colour caught her eye on the street outside. It was Finn, skating down the street just ahead of one of his friends, a pixie-blonde skater-girl . . . and Amelia had just leaned closer to the window to gaze after them, her look suddenly intent.

Yes! Olivia let out a silent cheer.

Amelia must have felt Olivia's eyes on her, though. She straightened, looking self-conscious. 'Sorry, I didn't catch that.' She yawned pointedly . . . but Olivia caught her sneakily glancing back at Finn and the skater-girl.

'Well,' Olivia said. 'If you don't want any spoilers for *Eternal Sunset* –'

'Are you kidding?' Amelia looked amused. 'No one can spoil the plot of *Eternal Sunset* for me. I've read it way too many times for that. It's the best of the Count Vira novels.' She reached into her bag to pull out an iPod and headphones.

Uh-oh. Time for my Hail Mary. Opening her mouth, Olivia prepared for her most last-ditch attempt of all – asking whether Amelia thought Josh was the type to read Count Vira books. *It might just work to make her look around at him . . .*

But before she could say a word, Amelia glanced back at the window . . . and froze.

Olivia peered over her shoulder. The skater-girl had caught up with Finn, and they were laughing together over some joke.

Amelia's face suddenly looked carved out of ice. She jerked her head away from the window – and glowered as she found Olivia watching her. 'Would you mind finding your own seat?' she said. She waved one hand in haughty dismissal. 'I'd like to be alone.'

Ohhh-kayy . . . Olivia opened her mouth, then closed it again. She had literally no idea what to say in response to that.

So much for my plan! Feeling as deflated as a limp balloon, she stood up . . .

And the bus screeched to a halt. 'That is it!' Mrs Martin swivelled around in her seat, pointing furiously at Olivia. 'If you stand up one more time in my bus, you will be walking the rest of the way to school. We'll see how you like it when you get detention for being late!'

'I'm sorry.' Hunching her shoulders, Olivia started back towards her original seat, feeling the bus driver's fuming gaze on her every step of the way.

At the last moment, though, inspiration struck. *I didn't manage to get Amelia to look at Josh . . . but I bet I could make Josh look at her!*

She veered off course to sit in the seat in front of Josh and his friends, just as the bus re-started with an angry-sounding roar of its engine. Olivia stumbled and almost fell into the seat, but it was worth it: she was exactly where she needed to be.

The more she thought about it, the more sense it made. Maybe Amelia wouldn't think twice about Josh, but she was certain she could plant the idea in *his* head.

Fixing a beaming smile on her face, she turned in her seat . . . and found Josh smirking at her. 'I knew it,' he drawled. 'Aren't you the girl who front-flipped in the hallway yesterday just to get my attention?'

Huh? Olivia stared at him. *What is he talking about?* She might be a former cheerleader, but she hadn't done a front-flip in months, much less in the school hallway. *Why would he think . . . ?*

Oh. She sighed. *If she looked like me, it must have been Ivy . . . and it sounds like something set off her vampire reflexes.* So much for keeping those hidden at school! 'Sorry,' she said. 'I'm that girl's sister.'

'Really?' Josh pulled a face. 'Geez, you two could be twins!'

Olivia had to call on all of her acting training to keep herself from letting out a cheer of triumph. *Foul, mean, and dumb . . . he's absolutely perfect!* There couldn't be a more Awful Alternative in their school. *Now all I have to do is bring them together.*

She glanced at the front of the bus, where Amelia was still sitting alone and looking out the window. *If I can just talk Josh into going up there and asking her out . . .*

Leaning across the top of her seat, she asked as casually as she could, 'So, are you seeing anybody?'

'Ha!' He burst into laughter. 'I knew it, I knew it, I knew it!' He shook his head and pointed straight at her, as his friends exploded into hilarity all around him. 'That moment you "bumped into" me – you were just faking, weren't you?'

'What?' Olivia's jaw dropped open. 'No! What – why –'

'You were just trying to get my attention!' He shook his head, still chortling. 'Listen, kiddo, I'm flattered, believe me, but I have a reputation to think about, y'know? I just can't date a ninth grader . . .' His gaze swept her up and down. 'Especially not one who looks like she's gone swimming in cotton candy!'

Ouch! Olivia snapped her jaw shut. Desperately, she fought to remember Jackson's acting tips on how not to blush. *Tongue behind my teeth; think of something cold* . . .

Maybe it would even have worked . . . if it hadn't been for what happened next.

'Hey, everyone!' The boy next to Josh cupped one hand to his mouth to call out to the rest of the bus. 'You should have heard it! This ninth-grade chick was just telling Josh how much she looooooves him!'

As the entire bus burst into laughter, and students all around her turned to point, Olivia sank back down into her seat. She could feel her skin burning, and there were no acting skills that could stop it.

Worse yet, while everyone else had turned to stare at the back of the bus, Amelia just kept looking out the window without turning around once. Her iPod must have drowned out all the noise. When the bus came to a halt a few minutes later, she walked straight to the door without glancing back for a single second at her Awful Alternative.

Olivia followed after with clenched teeth and hunched shoulders, while Josh's friends sent catcalls after her. This was definitely the last time she would *ever* take the Lincoln Vale bus!

As she marched through the hallway ten minutes later, Olivia did her best not to makc cye-contact with *anyone*. Seriously, had the kids from the bus *really* had to tell her embarrassing story to every single person they met today? She could hear whispers on every side, and she didn't need to have vampire hearing to know that they were talking about her.

I was trying to help this whole school with 'Operation Famelia'! she wanted to yell. *I was doing it for you guys!*

Instead, she kept her head down and her gaze fixed on the ground . . . until a strong hand suddenly grabbed her arm. Even as Olivia yelped, she was dragged sideways across the hallway floor. A moment later, a door slammed shut, closing her off from the crowded hallway. Shelves full of pens and paper rose around her.

'What on earth?' She whirled around. *Ivy!*

'What's going on?' Olivia asked her twin. 'And why are we in a stationery cupboard?'

'I should ask you that!' Ivy stared at her. 'Where have you been this morning? When I didn't see you on the bus, I thought you must be sick today.'

'Not . . . exactly.' Olivia sighed. At least the rumour mill hadn't reached Ivy yet. Maybe even the gossips were smart enough to know that the most popular girl in ninth grade wouldn't take well at all to people mocking her twin. 'I got the bus from Lincoln Vale.'

'Sorry?' Ivy frowned. 'But why –? No, never mind. I don't need any more of a headache!'

Olivia looked more closely at her sister. Ivy's skin was paler than usual, and her eyes looked shadowed. 'Why are we in a *stationery cupboard*?'

Ivy shrugged, looking miserable. 'I didn't know where else to go. I don't know *anything* at this crazy school! I walk into the hallways and just get overcome with the urge to . . . well, hide!' She slumped back against the shelves of paper, wrapping her arms around her chest defensively. 'I couldn't think of anywhere else we could talk without being interrupted.'

Olivia shook her head, concern overwhelming her earlier embarrassment. 'This has to stop,' she said. 'You can't *hide in cupboards* every day for four years, can you?'

'Maybe not,' Ivy muttered. 'But I also can't give fashion tips to every pale-faced, eyeliner-wearing ninth grader who thinks the Pall Bearers sold out . . . which they did not!' She straightened, her face darkening with obvious outrage. 'There's absolutely nothing wrong with keyboards, no matter what any of those goths want to say!'

'Ohh-kay,' Olivia said, and put her hands up.

'*I* didn't criticise your favourite band, though. Remember?'

'I know.' Ivy sagged again, the energy seeming to drain out of her. 'The thing is, I don't want to change just because of this popularity nonsense . . . but right now, I don't see how I can avoid it.'

Olivia reached out and took her sister's hand in hers. 'Maybe change is just inevitable,' she said quietly. 'I mean, look at us. We're older now, and we're in a new school, with new people all around us. Well . . .' she glanced over her shoulder 'new *stationery* around us, at the moment. But you know what I mean! We're going to have to change whether we like it or not.'

Ivy squeezed her hand even as she scowled. 'I wish I didn't have to.'

'Seriously?' Olivia couldn't help giggling as she imagined it. 'Are you telling me you want to be fourteen for the rest of your life, Ivy Vega?'

'Oh my darkness. No way!' Ivy shuddered, dropping Olivia's hand. 'That would mean I'd be trapped in this school in a time-loop forever and ever. Do you know how long *forever* is?'

'I know it's too long to spend in high school!' Olivia agreed. Their gazes met, and they both started laughing at once. Olivia darted forwards and wrapped her twin up in a hug. Ivy smelled of the incense she liked to burn, and she felt absolutely perfect to Olivia. 'It is so, so good to be talking with you again!'

'Even though it's one of the most surreal, ridiculous conversations ever?' Ivy's arms closed around her tightly.

'I only have these conversations with you,' Olivia said honestly. 'It's one of the reasons I love them.'

'Me, too. And we haven't been talking at all this week, have we?' Ivy sighed as she let go of the hug. 'I'm so sorry about what happened in the cafeteria the other day. It was just a situation that slipped completely out of my control. I didn't know what to do to fix it . . . and then everything got so weird after that.'

'Don't worry.' Olivia smiled reassuringly as she stepped back. 'It's all forgotten now. Honestly.'

'Are you sure?' Ivy's eyes looked dark and lost. 'Things have just gotten so tangled up –'

'Then we'll untangle them.' Olivia gave a firm nod. 'You're right, all of this nonsense has come to a head. Luckily, I'm here to help.'

Maybe Olivia didn't know how to handle Ivy's level of popularity . . . but she knew someone else who would. And Ivy and Olivia weren't the only ones who'd changed, this past year.

Ivy's eyes narrowed. 'I know that look. Olivia Abbott, what are you planning?'

'Don't you worry,' Olivia said, patting Ivy's

arm. Maybe she wouldn't be able to get Finn and Amelia together after all – but she could at least help her own sister. And it always felt better to have a plan of action!

'I know exactly what to do,' she announced. 'All that Hollywood training of mine is finally going to come in handy.'

'It is?' Ivy looked even more nervous than before. 'I'm not so sure . . .'

'*I* am,' said Olivia. 'All we need is an empty house – that'll be yours, tonight – and . . .' she braced herself, preparing for a trademark Ivy death-squint '. . . Charlotte Brown!'

'What?!' Ivy stared at her. 'Are you serious? You want to ask *Charlotte Brown* for help with this? The girl who ruled Franklin Grove Middle with a sparkly pink fist? She was our least favourite person there!'

'I can hardly believe it, either,' Olivia admitted,

'but . . . Charlotte may be our only hope at this stage. Can you think of anyone *more* qualified to give advice about popularity?'

'Oh, ack.' Ivy groaned. Her eyes darted furiously back and forth, as Olivia watched, holding her breath.

Finally, Ivy let out a heavy sigh. 'Fine,' she said. 'I've run out of ideas of my own . . . so I can't say no to any plan, no matter how much I hate it.' She set her jaw, looking as grim as if she were preparing to be marched to her own execution. 'Let's do it,' she said. 'Let's bring in Charlotte.'

Chapter Ten

The doorbell to Ivy's house rang that evening like a warning. She trudged towards it with heavy steps and found Charlotte Brown waiting for her on the porch, looking as pop-star wannabe as ever. The neat suburban lawns of Undertaker Hill were quiet and plain behind her, making Charlotte look even more glitzy by contrast. Her blonde hair was sprayed into perfect waves, and a bright pink leather purse, studded with rhinestones, hung over her arm. *All she's missing is a tiny little dog to ride in the purse!* Ivy thought.

'Ivy Vega.' Charlotte shook her head wonderingly as she looked Ivy up and down, from her black boots and combat trousers to her silver bat-wing top. 'If someone had said a year ago that you and I would be voluntarily *working together* on anything . . . would you have believed it?'

'Not in a million years.' Thinking of a thousand different snide comments Charlotte had tossed at her over the years, Ivy drew a deep breath – and then let it out in a *whoosh*, all her bad memories flooding out with it. 'But you know what? Since you helped us take down that awful Jessica Phelps last spring, I have *no* trouble believing it now. And that's all that matters.'

'Really?' Charlotte's lips quirked into a surprisingly shy-looking smile.

'Really,' Ivy agreed. Charlotte had helped save Olivia's big movie role – and her relationship with Jackson – from the schemes of Hollywood's most horrible vamp actress. That had to count for a lot. She stepped forwards. *Yes, this is really happening!*

Ivy was holding out her arms to Charlotte Brown, of all people . . . and Charlotte was doing the same in return. Franklin Grove Middle School's sworn enemies were *hugging*!

'Well.' Charlotte stepped back, patting her hair back into place. 'You've lucked out tonight. Not only am I working with you – I've brought reinforcements!'

'Huh?' Ivy followed the direction of Charlotte's pointing finger to look up the street. Then she grinned as she recognised the long blonde hair and hippie-styled clothing of the girl hurrying towards them. 'Holly!'

Holly Turner grinned back at Ivy as she reached the house. Her hair tumbled over her shoulders without a touch of hairspray, and embroidered flowers trailed all over her peasant blouse. 'Hey, Ivy. How's your new school going? Too bad you can't go to Willowton High with us!'

'Yeah, well . . .' Ivy was still trying to figure out how to answer that when her eyes nearly popped out – because Holly and Charlotte were exchanging an actual hug in front of her. *Whoa. That's two hugs for Charlotte in two minutes – and she looks like she's taking it for granted. Does enrolment at Willowton High come with a hug requirement?*

Ivy took a deep breath, absorbing the shock of it. *Maybe high school can be good for something after all!* Not only was Charlotte acting ten times nicer than she ever had before, but for the first time ever, she seemed to have actual friends – even friends who were visibly different from her – rather than just 'hangers-on'!

'Come on in,' Ivy said, as Holly and Charlotte

moved apart. Still feeling dizzy with surprise, she stepped back and waved them down the hallway. 'The others are all waiting in the kitchen.'

Holly had been to Ivy's house that summer, but this was the first time Ivy had ever invited Charlotte inside. She could feel the other girl looking at everything with curiosity, but there were none of the snide comments she would have expected a year ago. When they stepped into the kitchen, though, and found Olivia, Brendan, Sophia and Camilla waiting there, eating chips, Charlotte's eyes widened.

'Sophia! Your hair – it's like lightning!'

Sophia smiled serenely, munching on another chip. 'I know. Isn't it great?'

'Ah . . .' Charlotte swallowed visibly. 'Mm!' she said, through clamped-shut lips. 'Mmm!' Her face flushed as pink as the purse over her arm.

Ivy hid a smirk as she stepped up to Brendan's

side. Charlotte looked as if she were about to burst with the effort of restraining herself from giving her *real* opinion . . . but for once, Ivy's ex-nemesis was actually holding her nasty comments in. *I was right: high school has definitely been good for her!*

Olivia stepped smoothly into the breach before the moment could turn awkward. 'So, the reason we're all here . . .' she swept her gaze across the others, drawing everybody's attention '. . . is that Ivy's having a serious popularity problem.'

'Sorry?' Charlotte dropped the chip she'd just picked up. 'Did you say *Ivy*'s having a popularity problem?'

'You could say that again.' Ivy groaned. 'How do I get rid of it? Immediately?'

'Well . . .' Charlotte stared at her. 'Well . . .'

I think I just exploded Charlotte's head, Ivy thought ruefully. *Guess she didn't realise just how different our high school really is!*

'Sorry, cutie.' Brendan looped his arm around Ivy's shoulders, ignoring her mock-glare at the endearment. 'You're just too cool.'

'Whatever!' Ivy pretended to elbow him in the side.

'Ahem.' Olivia cleared her throat and gave them both a stern look, even as she patted Charlotte on the arm, obviously helping her through her shock. 'The point is, Ivy needs to get a handle on her popularity *without* being dishonest, or pretending to be someone she's not.' She turned to Charlotte. 'That's where you come in! Can you coach Ivy on how to deal with popularity without losing her temper?'

'Are you kidding?' Gathering herself together, Charlotte waved a dismissive hand. 'That will be *no* problem. Trust me, I'd mastered the art of Handling the Hallway by fifth grade!'

'Ohhh.' Ivy let out a breath as something

dawned on her. 'I *get* it now!'

'Sorry?' Olivia turned to stare at her.

'Nothing.' Ivy leaned over to grab another chip, trying to hide her expression. 'Sorry. I just meant, I'd really love the help.'

Privately, though, she was still reeling. She'd spent so many years loathing Charlotte for her 'mean girl' persona . . . but all that time, could Charlotte have been using it to keep her life manageable at Franklin Grove Middle School?

Was that why she said all those awful things?

Ivy swallowed hard as she remembered some of her own mean behaviour this past week, as she'd coped with her sudden popularity. Not only had she said some pretty nasty things herself to try to put people off, but there had been times when she had actually *meant* what she'd said.

Ouch. Ivy took a deep breath as she realised just how similar she and Charlotte might be after all. *But no one is un-saveable*, she told herself. *Not Charlotte . . . and not me, either.*

'Are you OK?' Olivia whispered, steering Ivy to one side as the others fell into a noisy debate about which movie this situation was most like. She frowned as she looked into Ivy's face. 'You look a little . . .'

'Unnerved?' Ivy gave a sad half-smile. 'I guess I am. I just never realised that if I were given half a chance . . . I might actually be even worse than Charlotte ever was.'

'Are you kidding?' Olivia gave her a quick, tight hug. 'You are my twin, Ivy Vega. Do you think I'd *ever* let you go that far?'

Ivy couldn't help laughing at that, even as she hugged Olivia back. 'Good point,' she said. 'You may look all pink and fluffy on the outside, but you're an unstoppable force on the inside. *No one* could stand against you for long.'

'That's right.' Nodding decisively, Olivia clapped her hands, breaking off the others' movie debate. 'Everyone! Let's have a dress rehearsal for the Hallway Gauntlet. Camilla? Will you direct? And Charlotte? For now, can you just stand back and watch how Ivy handles it? Then you can offer her advice on how to do it better.'

'Got it!' Camilla snapped to attention, her eyes sparkling under her latest velvet beret as she went into full-on Director Mode. Wiping off the crumbs from her hands, she jumped up from her seat. 'Sophia and Holly, you'll be the clingy goths. Brendan, you're the annoying skater-boy!'

'Liiiike, got it!' Brendan drawled. 'Totally, dude.'

Ivy rolled her eyes at him. It didn't help with the sudden sick tension in her gut, though. Even the thought of those hallways filled her with dread.

Camilla was still busy handing out the last of

her assignments. 'Olivia, you're the timid cheerleader who doesn't want to upset the cool girl.'

Olivia fluttered her eyelashes. 'How perfect!' she cooed.

Ivy groaned.

Camilla ignored them both. 'Everybody got it?'

'Got it!' they all chorused.

'Got it,' Ivy mumbled, a moment later than everybody else. Her shoulders sagged. Brendan gave her a sympathetic look before slouching off to take his place, carrying an imaginary skateboard by his side.

'Now!' Camilla pointed. 'Ivy? You stand by the front door. Everybody else, take your places along the hallway!' She mimed holding a clapperboard. Her voice switched to a movie narrator's rich tones. 'It's a normal morning at Franklin Grove High. Ivy's just about to step inside. Aaaand . . . take one!'

Her arm swung down. Obediently, Ivy stepped forwards . . . and was immediately swarmed.

'Iiiivy!' Sophia and Holly fluttered towards her, blocking her way. 'You are soooo cool! Won't you tell us how you did your hair? And your make-up? And your laces? And –'

'Um . . .' Smiling desperately, Ivy tried to side-step past them, but they wouldn't give her an inch of space. She could barely breathe as they clung closer and closer, filling up her vision.

'Wasn't the homework *boring?* What did *you* do last night, Ivy? Won't you tell us how to be like you? Ivy, Ivy, Ivy, Ivy . . .'

Panic made Ivy's heartbeat thrum against her skin. Her face twisted into a scowl, but they wouldn't step back. She couldn't escape. She couldn't breathe. She looked desperately to where Olivia waited, further down the hall, but her sister was too far away to help.

'Can we cut?' Charlotte asked sharply.

'Cut!' Camilla bellowed.

Grinning, Sophia and Holly high-fived each other and stepped back to await Charlotte's verdict.

The ex-head cheerleader was frowning intently. 'You can't do that thing with your face,' she told Ivy.

'What thing?' Ivy stared at her.

Charlotte shook her head impatiently. 'That squinty, I-hate-you face. That's too mean.'

'But they were smothering me!' Ivy protested.

'I know.' Charlotte rolled her eyes. 'Believe me, I know! But at most, you should look mildly annoyed.'

'Sorry?' Ivy shook her head wearily. 'I don't even know what that looks like!'

'Oh, for heaven's sake. Let me.' Charlotte swept past Ivy to take her place in the gauntlet, and Ivy was only too happy to step back.

There may have been a real Gauntlet at Wallachia Academy for vampires . . . but the Hallway Gauntlet at Franklin Grove High is infinitely worse.

Camilla counted down. 'Three . . . two . . . one . . . action!'

Walking briskly, Charlotte stepped into the hallway. Sophia and Holly swept down around her, shrieking with excitement.

'Ivy, Ivy, Iiiiivy!'

Huh. Ivy's eyes narrowed as she watched Charlotte's reaction. She stood listening, without trying to step past them, but her forehead was drawn into impatient lines. As she listened, she glanced down at her watch in a move that read clearly: *I have somewhere else I need to be!*

Without a word of prompting – or an I-hate-you face – Holly and Sophia started to clear a path for Charlotte to walk through.

'Oh. My. Darkness!' Ivy shook her head in disbelief. 'How did you *do* that?'

Charlotte shrugged. 'Just act like your time is *very* important, and the people around you will treat it that way! You don't have to be *mean*, or treat people badly – you just have to be honest about who you are . . . not the person other people think you should be.'

Charlotte's face softened. Looking rueful, she met Ivy's eyes directly. 'That is a lesson you helped *me* learn all through eighth grade.'

'Oh.' Ivy felt her own face soften. *Wow. There's one more thing I wouldn't have believed a year ago!* 'OK.' She blew out a breath. 'Can I try it again?'

Camilla nodded. 'Take your places, everybody,' she barked. 'We are back at the Hallway Gauntlet . . . take two!'

This time, Ivy felt a sense of purpose leading her as she stepped forwards. As Sophia and Ivy converged on her, she fought her instinctive panic, trying to remember Charlotte's advice. *Small, impatient frown . . . look at watch . . .*

Charlotte's voice rapped out. 'Can we cut?'

'Oh, fine. Cut!' Camilla sighed heavily. 'I'll bet real directors don't get *told* when to cut, though.'

Ivy didn't have any time to laugh. Charlotte was already hurrying towards her, and this time she reached out to physically push Ivy's posture into place. 'Shoulders straight and head up, that's all good, but *don't* raise your chin too much – you'll give yourself neck strain!'

'Seriously?' Ivy let out a half-laugh. 'Don't you think you might be getting a little too obsessive, now? I mean –'

'Why do you think I had to miss summer camp that one year?' Charlotte demanded.

'Um . . .' Ivy thought back. 'Oh, that's right, you *did* miss a year. Why –?'

'Because I was stuck at home wearing a neck brace, that's why!'

'Oh.' Ivy's eyes widened. *Wow.* 'OK,' she said. 'I'll keep my chin down.'

Who knew that popularity could actually give a girl physical injuries? I thought all I had to worry about was emotional damage!

'Try again,' Charlotte ordered.

Ivy nodded, rolling back her shoulders like a boxer getting ready to jump back into the ring. *I can do this*, she told herself. For the first time ever, it felt like it might actually be true.

She kept her shoulders back, her chin lowered, her eyes on her watch, her attitude impatient but not mean . . .

'And I'm through!' As she swept past Holly and Sophia in exactly the way that Charlotte had, Ivy let out a shout of triumph. 'I did it! Woot!' She punched the air.

'Ahem!' Camilla cleared her throat. 'You've made it past the *first* obstacle . . . You still have the annoying skater-boy *and* the timid cheerleader lying in wait!'

Uh-oh. Lowering her fist, Ivy looked around. *She's right.* Brendan was poised halfway down the hall, miming turning the wheels on his invisible skateboard. Olivia huddled near the end, her shoulders drawn up, holding a stack of textbooks in her arms as her eyes darted nervously around her.

'Oops.' Ivy sighed. 'OK. I'm ready.' She started forwards, trying to put herself back into Charlotte-mode . . .

And Camilla bellowed, 'Cut!'

'Sorry?' Ivy stared.

Camilla rolled her eyes under her beret. 'What on earth do you think you're doing, Vega? We need to run this scene through *from the top*!'

'What?!' Ivy's mouth dropped open. She turned slowly around . . . and found Holly and Sophia bouncing in place, getting ready to pounce all over again.

'Ohhhh, fine.' She sighed. 'I guess I can do it again. Probably.'

'Good,' Charlotte said. 'Because I have a few more notes.'

'Of course you do,' Ivy mumbled. *This is going to be a long evening.*

But as she took her position at the doorway, facing the full Hallway Gauntlet, with her twin giving her a surreptitious 'thumbs-up' gesture near the end of it, Ivy felt a sudden charge of energy run through her body. *Just look at all of them!*

The whole Franklin Grove Middle School gang was back together, for the first time since high school had begun – and with special new members in Holly and Charlotte! *This actually feels like old times. This is good!*

Ivy looked round at her friends and her sister, all gathered to help her. Her eyes stung even as she prepared to run the gauntlet all over again. *I know the old times can never really come back*, she thought, blinking back the would-be tears, *but it's nice to remember them . . . at least for a little while.*

Chapter Eleven

The next morning, it was time to put theory into practice. *This is not a drill.* Ivy took a deep breath as she stepped up to the main entrance of Franklin Grove High. The school bus had pulled away five minutes ago, and Brendan, Sophia and Olivia had all gone in ahead of her, giving her space to tackle the Hallway Gauntlet head-on.

She reached out for the door handle. Then she stopped. *Oh, come on*, she told herself. *Don't be a wimp! Remember how well it went last night?*

They'd run through the scene over a dozen times at her house, and even Charlotte had been impressed by the end of it. When they'd finished the final take, Camilla had announced, 'We have gold in the can!'

Ivy had barely understood a single word in that sentence, but at least it had sounded like a compliment. And even if it wasn't . . .

Right. She reached out and pulled the door open. *It's show time!*

Just as she'd practised, Ivy kept her gaze fixed on her locker up ahead, where Brendan, Olivia and Sophia were waiting. Before she could take two steps, though, two clingy goth-girls came racing towards her.

'Wasn't the homework *boring*, Ivy?'

'What did *you* do last night? I bet it was cool.'

'Of course it was cool. Ivy's *always* cool!'

'I wish I was like you, Ivy!'

Normally, Ivy would have panicked as they plucked at her sleeves and blocked her in every direction. This time, though, she had to restrain a burst of incredulous laughter. It was almost eerie how good Sophia and Holly's impression of these girls had been.

I think I've had this conversation before, Ivy thought. *Over a dozen times before, actually!*

Holding back a smile, she forced her forehead to crease. She glanced at her watch.

Almost imperceptibly, the two girls began to shift back, automatically starting to make space for her to leave, even as they kept on talking.

'Are you ready for the poetry reading in English?'

'I can't wait to hear what *you* chose!'

Ivy's mind went blank. Then she bit back a groan. *Oh, no! I was supposed to choose a poem to read today!* She'd been so busy doing her hallway homework, she'd forgotten all about finishing her English homework.

She shrugged, trying to look impatient instead of horrified. 'I'll have something by the time class starts.'

'Ooh.' The two girls fluttered back, eyes wide. 'You're *so* cool. I could never wing it so close to show time.'

'I've been agonising all week!'

'Oh, well, I'm sure it'll be fine.' Carefully keeping her nose – but *not* her chin! – in the air, Ivy walked forwards with subtle determination. *Just don't laugh!* she ordered herself.

It was hard not to laugh, though, as the two goths fell into a heated debate over their own poetry choices.

'Do you think I should have gone for "Angry Soul" instead of "Wilting Roses"?'

'All I know is, I'm going to *kill* with my choice: "Coffin of Confidence!"'

Looking at her watch, Ivy swept forwards . . .

and just like in the rehearsal, the goth-girls cleared a path.

Ivy let out a silent cheer. *I made it past Stage One! Now* . . . She slid a glance forwards. *Yup. It's time for Stage Two: the dumb skater-boy. Game on!*

One of Finn's friends took up most of the hallway ahead of her, sweeping out his arms and legs to show off his "killer" moves. 'And then I went – *whoosh!* – up that wall and I turned a flip like *this* . . .'

He flipped in mid-air and nearly knocked over two bunnies. *Remember your objective*, Ivy lectured herself as she started towards him. *Don't scowl, don't sigh, don't huff, don't . . . huh?*

Penny Taylor had just jumped in front of her, dressed in a very long black coat.

Wait a minute, Ivy thought. *This wasn't part of the script. I haven't rehearsed this!*

Penny's eyes looked huge with misery. Her

gaze skittered over three goths who were leaning against the wall of lockers nearby, obviously listening in, and her shoulders hunched. She whispered, 'Um . . . can I talk to you, Ivy? Please?'

Ivy gritted her teeth. *So much for the plan!* 'Oh, fine,' she muttered. 'If you must.'

Penny flinched as if she'd been slapped and Ivy winced, suddenly realising what she'd done. *Uh-oh. I wasn't supposed to be mean today!*

'Of course you can talk to me,' she said warmly. She wrapped one arm around Penny's shoulders, feeling the tension vibrating through the other girl. 'What's wrong?'

'It's just . . .' Penny slid her a nervous glance. 'You know our English class? This morning?'

'Yeah.' Ivy had to restrain herself from rolling her eyes. Was there *anyone* at this school who wasn't eager to remind her that she hadn't done her homework?

'Well . . .' Penny bit her lip. 'Did you have any particular Pall Bearers song in mind? To read?'

'Uh . . .' Ivy grimaced. 'Look, to be totally honest –'

'Oh, don't worry!' Penny's words rushed out as her eyes flew wide. 'I would never read the one you were planning on! No matter which one it is.' She grasped Ivy's arm with a feverish look in her eye. 'You know, I really won't read any of their lyrics if it's going to offend you. I would never do that!'

Gently, Ivy tried to detach Penny's fingers from her arm. 'Look, the Pall Bearers aren't really your thing, are they?'

'Of course they are!' Penny gave an anguished look at the watching goths. 'I mean, every goth loves the Pall Bearers, right? So, I do, too! It's just, I know you're a really big fan – I don't mind the keyboards either, by the way! – and I would never step on your toes. That's why I wanted to check.'

Ivy sighed. 'I'm not reading any of the Pall Bearers' lyrics, Penny. The whole CD collection is yours, free and clear.'

'Oh. Well. That's a relief, I suppose.' Penny's shoulders slumped. She stepped out from underneath Ivy's arms, looking more miserable than ever. 'So, I will read Pall Bearers lyrics, then.' She sighed. 'See you there?'

'Yup.' Ivy watched Penny walk away, goth-perfect in her long black trench coat . . . and slumped. She couldn't take this any longer. 'Penny?' she called out.

Penny froze, suddenly looking hopeful. 'Did you change your mind? Do you want to use one of their songs after all?'

'That's not it,' Ivy said. She glanced at all the other students watching them from around the hallway. 'Could you just come back here for a second? Please?'

As Ivy waited for Penny, she heard her friends down the hall hissing at each other in sudden panic:

'What is she doing?'

'She's going off-script!'

'Improvising was NOT part of the plan!'

'Chill, guys,' Ivy whispered. She knew Olivia wouldn't be able to hear her, but Brendan and Sophia both would, with their vampire hearing. 'I know what I'm doing.'

At least, I hope so, she added silently.

Penny came to a halt in front of her, quivering with nerves. 'Y-yes? Was there something you wanted, Ivy?'

'Yes,' Ivy said. She looked her in the eye. 'I want to know: do you *really* want to read the Pall Bearers' lyrics?'

Penny blinked rapidly. 'I thought you said I could! You said –'

'Don't get me wrong,' Ivy said. 'The Pall Bearers *suck* – I mean, they *rule* – but you don't have to read one of their songs just because that's what you think you *should* do. You know that, right?'

Penny looked around at the watching goths. Ivy could almost see the wheels turning in her head.

'But if I don't . . .'

'Look,' Ivy said, dropping her voice to a whisper. 'The whole idea of Mr Russell's assignment is to read something you connect with, emotionally, on a personal level. We both know the Pall Bearers aren't *it* for you, right?'

Penny's eyes dropped. 'Right,' she whispered. 'I mean, I don't think they're *bad*, I just . . .'

'They're just not *your* thing.' Ivy nodded.

'So if you go up and read those lyrics, you're not going to get as "into" them as everyone expects, are you? That means people are going to have *questions*.' She laid one hand on Penny's stiff shoulder, feeling a wave of empathy. Ivy, of all people, knew exactly how hard it was to pretend to be a different kind of person. 'Don't you think it would be better to give them questions you can actually answer?' she asked gently.

For a moment, Penny just looked down at her feet. Then her chin rose. She met Ivy's gaze. 'Do you remember that poetry book I was reading at the skatepark?'

Ivy frowned. 'That was while you were pretending to be a goth, wasn't it?' she whispered. 'I'm not sure that book is the best –'

'No!' Penny said. 'There's one poem in there I *really* loved. Genuinely. "Shadows in Sunshine." *That*'s the one I'd pick if I really could.'

'"Shadows . . ."? Ohhh, yeah.' Ivy's eyebrows rose. 'I remember that one.' *And actually* . . .

Yeah, it was moody – but it was pretty, too. And the more she thought about it, the more she could see: it really would have meaning for Penny, the goth who secretly loved pink.

'That sounds like a great choice,' she said truthfully.

'You think so?' Penny's lips curved into a smile of delight. 'Then I'm going to do it!'

'Fantastic.' Ivy gave her shoulder one last squeeze, then stepped away. As she made her way briskly down the hallway, she barely even remembered that she was running the dreaded Hallway Gauntlet. Warmth filled her chest, making her feel light as air.

She bypassed the annoying skater-boy without giving him a glance, even as his backflip landed him so close to her that he actually apologised, backing away with his hands held up defensively. *Maybe he thinks I'm going to go after him the way I went after that idiot in the trench coat*, Ivy thought, and rolled her eyes. *Honestly, I'm not that scary!*

When the bunny girl with six piled textbooks scurried past, Ivy gave her a half-smile. The bunny girl stopped in her tracks, staring. 'Um . . . um . . .' She licked her lips, looking panicked. 'I . . .'

'Yes?' Ivy asked gently. She stopped to listen.

'What are you doing?' Sophia whispered. The sound carried down the hallway to Ivy's sensitive hearing.

Ivy ignored her friend's question. Instead, she waited patiently for the bunny girl to work up her courage.

Finally, the girl gave Ivy a shaky smile. 'Hi,' she said. 'I'm Julia.'

'Nice to meet you, I'm Ivy.'

The bunny girl beamed, looking almost relieved as she continued walking down the hall. 'Wow,' the girl whispered to herself, not realising that Ivy could hear her. 'She's *not* scary!'

Nope, Ivy thought. *And maybe I don't need to be, either.*

As Ivy joined her friends by her locker a few minutes later, she was smiling as broadly as Julia. She'd successfully run the Hallway Gauntlet . . . and she knew she'd never be afraid of it again.

Chapter Twelve

Olivia couldn't have been happier for her twin . . . but now that Ivy had finally learned how to manage the dreaded hallway, it was time for Olivia to focus on her other mission: *Get Famelia together – for the whole school's sake!*

As she headed for her locker on the other side of school, leaving Ivy and her other vamp friends behind, Olivia could actually feel the difference in people's reactions. While goths and bunnies both stared at Ivy and everyone around her, Olivia turned into the Invisible Girl the moment she stepped out of Ivy's charmed circle. *There should be a loudspeaker warning every time I walk away from Ivy*, she thought ruefully, as she stepped back to make way for a noisy group of goths. *Warning! Warning! You are now leaving the popularity zone!*

The goths passed by her without a second look . . . and Olivia smiled, relaxing into her anonymity. *Jackson was right. This could be a whole lot worse.*

Honestly, it was going to be weird enough to alternate between weeks of normal high school and weeks of Hollywood filming across the next several months. But if she wanted to stay grounded through it all – and keep herself from becoming a nightmarish diva like Jessica Phelps – this was exactly what she needed to keep her steady. She had Hollywood ceremonies and film sets to make her feel special . . . and school to keep her normal and anonymous.

This feels right, she decided. *Now all I have to do*

is get Operation Famelia moving again!

Olivia nibbled at her lower lip. She'd barely slept last night for wondering what she should do next to help Finn and Amelia get together. This morning, though, she was pretty sure she had the perfect plan.

All she needed was a box of chocolates and a yellow umbrella, and she'd . . .

Oh, no. Trouble ahead!

Just ahead of Olivia, Amelia was stepping backwards from her locker – and she was obviously completely unaware that another student had set a big, bulky bag just behind her. The Queen of Goth was about to take a nasty fall.

'*Look out!*' Olivia yelled.

But Amelia's boot had already landed askew on the bulky bag. She started to fall, her arms pinwheeling . . .

. . . and from out of nowhere, Finn zoomed

down the hall on his skateboard. Moving so swiftly it almost looked like he was flying, he sped towards Amelia and caught her in mid-air before she could hit the ground.

Amelia gasped, grabbing on to him and clinging to his shoulders as his board screeched to a stop. Finn's arms locked around her waist. As Olivia watched, open-mouthed, his head lowered towards Amelia. The Goth-Queen's eyes drifted closed as her head tipped back, obviously waiting for his kiss . . .

And Mr Russell's voice snapped through the air.

'That's it!' Looking triumphant, the English teacher marched down the hall. 'It's detention for you this time, Mr Jorgensen. You've been told before about skateboarding inside the school!'

Not now! Olivia pleaded silently. But it was too late.

Groaning, Finn let go of Amelia. She stepped

back hastily, brushing herself down and not meeting his gaze. Without a word of protest, Finn scooped up his skateboard and followed after Mr Russell, all the way to Principal Carson's office.

Olivia shook her head despairingly as she watched him disappear behind the closed door. Then she looked back at Amelia . . . and began to smile.

The Goth-Queen was still gazing after Finn as if no one else in the world existed.

Talk about a perfect 'Meet Cute' moment! Olivia bit her lip to hold back a burst of delighted laughter as she sidled up to Amelia. 'That was quite heroic, wasn't it?' she murmured. 'The way he saved you . . .'

'Sorry?' Amelia seemed to snap out of a daydream. Her face tightened, as if she were preparing some sharp remark . . . but then she sagged. 'Yeah,' she said softly. Her eyes turned back to the closed door of Principal Carson's office. 'I guess it was.'

Yes! Olivia wanted to do a high-jump of triumph. Instead, she opened her mouth, already preparing her next move. She knew exactly what to say next: *No other boy would have done what Finn did!*

But Principal Carson's office door opened before she could say a word.

'This is outrageous!' Mr Russell burst out, red-faced, and stalked down the hallway, scattering students in his wake.

Behind him, Finn and the principal stepped out together . . . and they were both smiling!

What on earth is going on? Olivia wondered, freezing halfway to her locker.

As she watched, Finn and Principal Carson shook hands. Then Finn started walking . . . straight towards Amelia.

The whole hallway went silent as everyone gathered around, eyes wide.

Amelia waited in front of her locker, and for once, the Goth-Queen looked anything but cool. One hand fluttered up to touch her hair. Her other hand closed around her locker door. Olivia could see Amelia's chest rising and falling, as if she were breathing quickly.

Finn came to a halt in front of her, grinning, his blond hair falling over his shoulders and his blue eyes intent. 'So,' he said. 'I just agreed on a new plan with Principal Carson. You know how I've been doing some volunteering with kids, teaching them how to skateboard?'

'Um . . . yeah?' Amelia raised her eyebrows, obviously trying to look bored. It didn't work. Her fingers visibly tightened on the door of her locker.

Finn's grin widened. 'Well, Carson says I

can do something like that here, too. I'll be giving lunchtime lessons in the skatepark to any students who are interested. And the thing is . . .' He paused, running one hand through his hair and starting to look nervous for the first time. 'The thing is, I need someone to manage the programme, and, well, I've seen you hanging out at the skatepark a lot. So . . .' He spread out his hands questioningly. 'Would you be interested in joining me?'

Eek! This is perfect! Olivia could barely stop from hugging herself in delight. *Asking her to help him with his skateboarding? He might as well be asking her on a date!*

She wanted to shout 'YES!' on Amelia's behalf. It took everything in her to firmly button up her lip. *No more meddling, remember? Just please, please let her make the right decision! She* will *make the right decision . . . won't she?*

The whole hallway was silent, waiting, as Amelia looked down at the linoleum squares on the floor, a crease forming in her forehead. Finn's smile wavered. Olivia panicked.

Uh-oh. She surely can't say no . . .

As she watched, Amelia chewed on her black-lipsticked lip, frowning harder. Finn's smile disappeared. He started to step back.

Then Amelia looked up, let go of her locker, and held out her hand. 'Shake on it,' she said. 'I'm in!'

'Yes!' Finn's face broke into the biggest smile Olivia had ever seen as he grabbed Amelia's hand . . . but not to shake it. Instead, he yanked her forwards into a hug.

And Amelia threw her arms around him to hug him back!

Gasps sounded all around them. Goths, skaters and bunnies all stared in shock. A small smattering of applause broke out – then quickly died.

Uh-oh. Olivia snuck a covert look around . . . then started grinning. No one seemed to be really offended by 'Famelia' after all – they were just completely baffled by the concept!

Finn and Amelia didn't seem to have any trouble with it, though. And the complete incomprehension on everyone else's faces as Finn swung Amelia round in a spinning hug was actually pretty hilarious . . . especially as the closest students all had to scramble backwards to avoid being hit by Amelia's flying feet!

The looks on Finn's and Amelia's faces, as he awkwardly set her down, were just adorable.

Olivia let out a happy sigh. *Maybe it'll take time, but everyone will come around in the end*, she decided, looking at the gathering of shocked faces. *And then we'll see how strong the barriers between people at this school really are!*

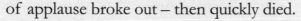

Finn only seemed to notice his observers as he set Amelia down. 'Um, I'm so – pleased,' he said hastily, and shot a look back at his staring skater friends. 'I mean, because we'll need your organisational skills.'

'Oh, yeah?' Amelia asked. She was grinning, too, for the first time since Olivia had met her. 'You've noticed my skills?'

'Absolutely,' Finn said. 'I've seen the way you keep your gang of friends together. You're the best!'

Amelia didn't say a word. But she was blushing with delight . . . and as her gaze caught Olivia's, Olivia couldn't help giving the Goth-Queen a fat wink.

Amelia's blush deepened.

'So, we'd better work out the details, right?' Finn held out his hand to Amelia. 'Maybe in the library?'

'Sounds good to me,' Amelia said. Holding her head high, she took Finn's hand and they walked together through the whispering, staring crowd.

Mr Russell emerged from his classroom just long enough to snarl: 'No skating in the corridors, remember!'

'I remember.' Finn raised his free hand in casual acknowledgement, rolling his eyes.

He isn't even carrying his skateboard! Olivia thought indignantly. But the Skater King was clearly too ecstatic to worry about even the most annoying of teachers right now.

As the couple passed Olivia, Amelia pulled Finn to a stop. 'You know,' she said sheepishly to Olivia, 'you're not so bad, for someone who thinks that pink goes with everything!'

Olivia grinned happily up at the older girl. 'It really does!'

Amelia's lips twitched. Her free hand reached out as if to pat Olivia on the arm. Then she pulled back, as she obviously reconsidered. Instead, she gave Olivia a small smile and a nod, turned back to Finn, and continued down the hall.

'So . . .' Olivia started at the sound of Ivy's voice. She was sidling up to her. 'Your matchmaking worked, huh?'

'It *so* worked!' Olivia bounced on her toes with delight. 'Did you see how happy they looked together? Of course, I can't take all the credit, but maybe I could work on my skills. I just need to develop a lighter touch. Hmm . . .'

Her gaze moved around the corridor, moving from boy to girl. 'Maybe, next time . . .'

'No way!' Ivy's hand clamped around her arm. 'That's enough matchmaking for now. I want us both to have a quiet life for the rest of the semester! Just the two of us hanging out without any interruptions or drama or –'

'A quiet life?' Olivia let out a snort of disbelief as she turned to stare at her twin. 'For a whole semester? Are you insane, Ivy Vega? That stuff never happens to us!'

'Well . . .' Ivy grinned, shaking her head. 'You may have a point. We don't seem to "do" quiet lives, do we?'

'Absolutely not,' Olivia agreed, smiling in satisfaction. 'And that's just right for us.'

Maybe they'd both had a few hiccups as they'd settled into their new school – but from now on, she was determined to make the most of it. *Together.*

She linked arms with her sister to walk together to their next class in perfect comfort. No groupies got in their way, no one tried to squeeze in between them or make any nasty comments about Olivia's clothes . . . and when Olivia glanced back over her shoulder, her eyes widened with delight.

Behind them, students were beginning to mingle! Goth-girls were asking if they could borrow bunny girls' magazines during lunch. Skaters were joking with goths. She could see at least four smiles that were less secretive than they would have been the day before, and also some upward nods of the head.

The blossoming romance between Finn and Amelia was *already* making a real difference to the school. 'You know,' Olivia said to her twin, 'I have a feeling we're both going to be really happy here, from now on . . .'

Ivy would have shared her sister's satisfaction . . . if she hadn't been so nervous about what was coming next.

As Mr Russell stalked into place in front of the class, she could see that he still hadn't recovered from the disappointment of Finn's triumph with Principal Carson. His face was still flushed, and his eyes glittered with frustration as he glared around the room.

'Right!' he said. 'The moment has arrived. It's time for you *all* to read out your poems.'

Ivy slumped in her seat, wishing that she could disappear. *What am I going to do? I haven't chosen anything yet!*

It was great that for the first time ever, she was actually sitting next to her own twin in class. But that wouldn't do her much good when she got a failing grade!

Her English teacher paced back and forth in front of the room with quick, impatient steps. 'The reason I set you this assignment is because poetry has a way of revealing things about people . . .'

Ouch. Ivy turned to glance at Penny, who was sitting two desks behind her. Their gazes met . . .

and then they both looked away quickly.

'. . . and because high school English is *very* different from middle school English,' Mr Russell declared, 'a student's feelings are *just* as important as his or her intelligence now. To truly engage with the texts you will read, you must *feel* them in your hearts!' He spun around on one heel. 'So! Who will *reveal themselves* first?'

Uh-oh. Ivy gulped. *Talk about pressure!*

A nervous hush fell over the class. All around the room, students ducked down, hiding their gazes.

It looks like nobody wants to read their poems now, Ivy thought. *And no wonder!* No matter what poems anyone had chosen, all everyone else in class would be thinking about was hidden meanings. *What is Mr Russell thinking? This is almost mean.*

Ivy slouched even lower in her chair.

Mr Russell let out an impatient sigh. 'Fine! I'll choose randomly, then.' He snatched the roll call list off his desk and glanced down at it. 'Penny Taylor. You'll go first.'

Penny gasped, clutching the anthology close to her chest. She was still wearing her long black trench coat, and her bone-white face looked almost sickly beside the black cloth now.

'Don't be shy, Miss Taylor.' Mr Russell rolled his eyes. 'It's just reading a few lines, remember? You might as well take your place in front of the class and get it over with.'

Penny nodded weakly. But she looked glued to her chair.

This is all my fault, Ivy realised.

'Shadows in Sunshine' was a poem *loaded* with personal meaning for Penny – meaning that everyone would pick up on and gossip about at lunch, if things went wrong! And if they did . . .

Ivy's mouth suddenly felt dry. All she'd tried to do was help Penny to be herself. Now, she feared that she had pushed too hard. If Penny became an object of ridicule because of her poem – the poem Ivy had encouraged her to choose – Ivy would never forgive herself. But what could she do?

Before she'd even made any conscious decision, she felt her hand shooting up in the air.

'Yes, Miss Vega?' Mr Russell sighed. 'Do you have something you wish to contribute?'

'Yes, I do,' Ivy said firmly. 'Penny was only hesitating, sir, because we were planning to read a poem together.' She saw Penny's eyes widen. She gave the other girl an encouraging smile. 'Would that be OK?'

Mr Russell raised his eyebrows. 'That sounds not only "OK", but excellent! Why don't you both step up to the front of the class?'

Ivy jumped up, and Penny followed, still looking nervous. As they reached the front of the class, Penny opened the textbook with trembling fingers.

'Every other verse?' Ivy whispered.

Penny nodded silently. As she looked down at the textbook, though, her expression smoothed. Her voice was strong as she read the first line, and real feeling sounded in her words.

'I sit surrounded by a crowd of people,
But none of them are looking at me . . .'

She really does love this poem, Ivy realised.

Every eye in class was on them as they passed the verses back and forth. They worked surprisingly well as a team but Ivy was thrilled to notice by the end of the poem that far more eyes were on Penny than on her! *She really is an amazing reader.*

'. . . and shadows in sunshine are my home.'

Penny's voice throbbed with emotion as she finished.

Everyone in class burst into applause. Penny's face lit up as she looked around, taking it all in. *Thank you*, she mouthed to Ivy.

Ivy shook her head, smiling. 'It was all you,' she whispered back.

'That was absolutely captivating!' Mr Russell leaped from his chair. All of his earlier irritation with Finn seemed to have been swept away by his excitement. 'I've learnt so much about both of you from that reading!'

Uh-oh. Ivy traded a look with Penny. *What is that supposed to mean?* 'You know . . .' she began, hoping for a distraction.

But there was no stopping their English teacher now. 'What bravery!' he declared, as he began to pace the room. 'The two of you chose to celebrate your differences – *not* something that happens often in high school! There's far too much value given to "fitting in" here. Bravo for a pair of friends who can admire each other for exactly what makes them each unique!'

Um . . . Raising her eyebrows, Ivy glanced at Penny's long trench coat and dyed black hair. *I don't think many people would see the differences between us right now. Maybe Mr Russell is just super-perceptive?*

Luckily, the class seemed to take their cue from Mr Russell's enthusiasm. They all applauded again as the girls walked to their desks, Penny leading the way – and Ivy beamed as she saw other students offering Penny high-fives.

Just as Ivy slipped into her seat, she saw

Penny come to a halt in front of her own. The other girl paused, taking a deep breath. Then she unbuttoned her coat, and took it off.

Ivy's jaw almost hit her desk.

Beneath the coat, Penny wore a sky-blue dress that Olivia would die for! And as the black trench coat slipped away, Ivy saw the tension drain from Penny's expression.

As Penny sat down she looked pretty, confident and more relaxed than ever before. *No wonder*, Ivy thought. *For the first time ever, she isn't pretending to be someone she's not!* As everyone watched, Penny clasped her hands together and smiled.

Admiring whispers broke out all around them.

'She looks fabulous!' a bunny girl whispered to her friend, near the windows. 'Where do you think she found that dress?'

At the same time, on the other side of the

classroom, a goth-girl murmured, 'I didn't know Penny was so cool!'

'Well,' the girl's friend said authoritatively, 'it's *always* cool when someone is *real.* Don't you think?'

Absolutely, Ivy thought. Beaming, she sat back in her seat. *Mission accomplished . . . in every way!*

Not only had she learned how to handle her own popularity, but she had successfully off-loaded some of it on to Penny – *without* forcing Penny to pretend to be someone she wasn't.

Ivy looked at Olivia sitting beside her – exactly where she belonged – and smiled.

Maybe I can cope with high school after all!

Ivy was still beaming hours later, as she wandered towards the school bus with Olivia, Brendan and Sophia.

'Ohhh!' Bouncing with excitement, Olivia tugged on Ivy's arm. 'Just look at that!' She pointed across the field to where Amelia and Finn sat with their heads close together, studying a timetable. 'Isn't that sweet? They're planning their classes together!'

Ivy grinned and rolled her eyes. 'I'm just glad they're in a higher grade than us, so I won't have to avert my eyes five times a day!'

'Oh, hush,' Olivia said, giving Ivy a nudge. 'You know you're a romantic at heart!'

Ivy was still laughing as she stepped on to the bus . . . then stopped. *Wait a minute.*

No one was making space for her! Every seat in front of her was full – and no one was leaping up to give up their seat, the way they had every day so far. *What's going on?* she wondered.

Brendan snickered and nudged her shoulder. 'Doesn't it feel great to be invisible again?'

Ivy blinked. She looked around with a new perspective. 'You know what, it really does!'

She grabbed a handrail and held on as the bus pulled away from Franklin Grove High. All around, other students were shouting and throwing things at each other. A screwed-up ball of paper accidentally hit Ivy on the cheek. She froze, waiting . . .

. . . And *no one* apologised!

As the bus drove down the road, Ivy touched the spot on her cheek where thc ball of paper had hit her, and she smiled.

She'd never been happier in her life.

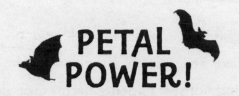

PETAL POWER!

Readers, when you think about the best in bunny fashion, who springs to mind? A young lady who has stepped out on the red carpet, who's danced at the prom in a pink rhinestone cowboy hat, and who knows everything there is to know about gingham? Me, too – it's our favourite friend-to-vampires, Olivia Abbott!

In this issue of VAMP, Olivia has agreed to share some of her unique fashion tips. Her only demand was that we allowed her to use pink rhinestones. Of course we agreed!

So, all you vamps out there, gather your materials and get ready to channel your inner bunny. Olivia Abbott is in town to show you how to turn heads by making your very own special flower accessory.

Signing off,

Georgia Huntingdon, Editor in Chief

Ever since I saw the rose petals that decorated the ballroom in Transylvania, and discovered the super-romantic vampire legend of the Free Rose of Summer, I've had a real thing about flowers. And not just pink flowers – they're great in every colour!

So, here's my top tip for bringing a floral touch to your own outfit, by adding a homemade flowery headband. And yes, there might just be the odd pink rhinestone included . . .!

Materials Needed

- Templates of flowers and leaf (supplied here)
- Slim, plain hairband
- Green felt
- Scraps of stiff flower-printed cotton of felt in different colours
- Embroidery thread and needle
- Fabric scissors
- Cute buttons
- Pencil
- Glue
- Pink rhinestones or glitter

Instructions

- Trace the three different-sized flower templates on to a piece of paper and cut them out.

- Now choose three different scraps of fabric (or felt if you prefer) and place a flower shape on top of each of them. Draw round the flower shapes with a pencil and cut them out carefully using fabric scissors.

- Trace your leaf template on to a piece of paper and cut it out. Place the leaf shape on top of your green felt and cut out, following the edges of the template.

- Place your green felt leaf down on your work surface, then arrange your three flowers on top of it, with the smallest shape on top.

- Pick out a cute button and place it on top of your arrangement.

Awesome! You should have something that looks like this:

Now it's time to sew the flower together. Make sure you get an adult to help you. Needles are nearly as sharp as Ivy's fangs are when she's forgotten to go to the dentist!

- Thread a needle and sew the button to your flower, looping your thread between the holes of the button and making sure you pierce through all of the layers.

- After you've sewn through the button holes several times, tie your thread in a knot right at the back of your work and cut off the excess thread, close to the knot.

You've just created the most beautiful flower! You can make some more, or keep it simple with just one. (My step-mom Lillian always says less is more. But I don't know about that!)

- Now, take your hairband. You'll need to prop it up between two heavy books or two stable containers so that the top of the hairband is nice and secure.

- Apply a few drops of glue to the back of your flower and stick it on to the hairband, wherever you think it will look prettiest. Add the other flowers if you've made more than one.

- Now take your pink rhinestones and carefully glue them along the rest of the hairband. You could even add some rhinestones to the petals of your flower, for extra sparkle.

- Leave overnight for the glue to set.

That's it! You have just created a hair accessory that is totally unique and totally bunny. Yeehaw!